D ead-Eye awoke, startled.

    Something wasn't right. He could sense it. He heard soft, restless noises coming from the animals at the edge of the clearing. The mule was skittish. The black Morgan, however, stood stark still and on guard. In the darkness, Dead-Eye saw the horse's eyes glow crimson, like the tip of a hot poker, and, when he snorted, heat and cinder were expelled.

"Brimstone," he whispered. "What is it, boy?"

Nearby, something howled. Not a dog. Something much bigger and much more fierce in nature. The sound rose skyward, echoing off canyon walls, sweeping through the naked branches of leafless trees. It was a guttural, bestial sound etched with savagery and brutal intent.

Dead-Eye drew his revolver and cocked the hammer.

"What was that?" exclaimed Job, popping up out of the warm folds of his blankets like a child's jack-in-the-box.

The creature howled again. Louder. Closer.

The gunfighter's good eye narrowed. The blind eye cast a pale glow upon the snowy ground of the clearing. "Company's coming."

The Saga of

DEAD-EYE

BOOK TWO
Werewolves, Swamp Critters & Hellacious Haints

by RONALD KELLY

Book Two: Werewolves, Swamp Critters,
& Hellacious Haints
is dedicated to the following folks:
Hunter Goatley
Alex McVey
Tod Clark
Dawn Shea and
Stephen Groves

Chapter One

On the Banks of the Mississippi River
Western Tennessee
November 1866

Willie Prewitt lashed out with a cane pole, casting his line into the churning, red current of the Mississippi River. It was a nasty business, fishing was; not a pleasurable, relaxing pastime as it once was, but a repulsive chore to be endured. The only positive aspect of Old Man River turning to blood was that the fish found it just as incomprehensible as the river folks did and were downright eager to escape the watery depths they had once called home.

Willie's line grew taut and he hauled his fifteenth catfish of the morning from the crimson flow. The poor thing thrashed wildly, its gills clotted and engorged with congealed sludge. It was literally choking, gasping for air. The red-headed boy dunked it in a wooden bucket of spring water to rinse it off, then tossed it into a pile in the dry, withered grass nearby.

"Looks like you're quite the fisherman, boy," said a voice behind him.

The twelve-year-old glanced over his shoulder. Two men sat on mounts, appraising his skill with a rod and line. One sat tall on a coal-black Morgan, while the other straddled a mule as white as a winter's snow.

They were a peculiar pair. The one on horseback was tall and lanky, dressed in a dusty black frockcoat and trousers, white silk shirt, string tie, and a low-crowned black hat. He didn't look at all well. In fact, the pale pallor of his gaunt face in stark contrast to his thick black mustache and hair gave him the appearance of a man near death or well past that point.

Willie recalled his own Grandpa Prewitt at his wake the year before. The elderly corpse had looked more alive lying stone-cold dead in his casket than this fellow did sitting astride his horse. Two things about the man interested Willie the most. One was the blind, yellow eye that almost seemed to cast a glow within the sunken socket on the left side of his face. The other was the big .44-caliber Colt Dragoon—nickel-plated with ivory grips—that was holstered, crossways, across his slender belly.

The other man—the one who rode the mule—was as opposite of the first man as anyone could possibly be. He was negro in race, short and wiry, and wore a gray derby hat atop his bald head. His dark face wore a wry expression and the teeth in his smile were a picket of silver and gold. He wore a sleeveless vest with more pockets than the boy had ever seen one man boast before, a collarless shirt, woolen britches, and mule-eared boots that reached all the way to his knees. Several necklaces of charms and trinkets were looped around his neck; a mummified chicken's foot, the feathers of three different birds—eagle, owl, and buzzard, from the looks of them—and three small glass bottles linked together with a silver chain. He had never seen such objects before, but sensed that they had to do with dark magic and conjuring.

It was the little black man who had spoken to him, so he answered back. "Not really. The way the river is now, those fish are right anxious to get clear of it. They'd pert near jump onto the bank themselves, if they could muster the gumption to do so."

A dark mood seemed to shadow the little man's eyes. "When did this happen? The river turning to blood and all?"

"Two days ago. It was as muddy as a hog wallow in the morning, then as bloody as a drunken knife-fight in a saloon that afternoon. Got no inkling how it got that way."

The look in the black man's brown eyes told Willie that he probably had a good idea.

"Ain't it a bit cold for you to be sitting out here on the bank for hours at a time, young'un?" asked the tall fellow in the black broadcloth suit. The man's good eye narrowed as he studied the boy's face, for there was something there that shouldn't have been.

Embarrassed, Willie turned his head a bit, hiding his right cheek. "Ain't got no choice, mister," he told him. "My pa came home from the skirmish in Gettysburg missing a leg and half his right arm. I'm the provider now. Gotta hunt, fish, and trap most every day to keep my family fed."

"Would there be a ferry nearby?" asked the gunslinger.

"About a mile and half north of here. Old Man Caruthers has a sawmill there. He carries folks across the river on a flatboat for a fee."

"Much obliged, young man." The mojo man dug something from a vest pocket and flipped it his way.

The boy caught the object in mid-air and was shocked to find he was holding a twenty-dollar gold piece. "No sir! I can't take this. It's a fortune... my papa would tan my hide if I brought it home. We ain't folks to be pitied."

"It ain't pity I'm offering, child, but respect. You take that into town and buy dry goods for the winter: beans, flour, lard, coffee. And winter shoes for you and your brothers and sisters, if'n you have any."

"Got three of each kind," Willie told him. The boy struggled in his mind for a reason to deny the gift. "It just ain't right, me taking such a thing."

The little man in the derby hat leaned forward, hands braced on the horn of his saddle. "Boy, pride has killed many a man, either with bullets or starvation. Now, you pick up those fish and take them home, and then go fetch those things I suggested. Your ma and pa might bristle at the charity at first, but they'll think better of it later on."

The red-headed boy nodded and smiled gratefully. "Much obliged, Mister...?"

"Job," the little man replied. "Like that woe begotten feller in the Bible. And this here's Dead-Eye."

The tall man in black clothing nodded somberly. He continued to stare grimly, unable to pull his gaze free. "Son... who did that to you?"

Willie Prewitt's ears reddened in shame, as did the ugly, twisted scar on the side of his face that ran just below his right eye clean down to the corner of his mouth. "It was a Union man, before Papa came home from the War. Rode onto the farm with a battalion of men and took food and all they could carry. He beat my ma and bred with her against her will. That's how my baby sister came about. When I tried to stop him, he carved his initials in my face." He laid a hand gently against the deep crisscrossing ruts of furrowed flesh. "GH" had been scrawled there with the tip of a bayonet in a bold and violent hand. "He was right proud of that name of his, the onery bastard. Spouted it every chance he got."

Dead-Eye's face grew rigid. "And that name... what would it be?"

The boy scowled, as though swallowing a generous spoonful of castor oil. "Garland Hughes."

The tall man nodded slowly, as though digesting the two words, committing them to memory. Lodging them deep down in his brain, to fester and cultivate contempt.

Willie Prewitt watched as the two rode past and headed northward along the bank of the river. His encounter with the two had been unexpected and a tad disturbing at first, but had yielded good will and a chance for survival. Curiously, he bit the edge of the Liberty Head coin to determine whether it was real or not. The twenty-dollar gold piece nearly chipped his teeth and he knew, for a fact, that what he held was a genuine blessing.

Chapter Two

Caruthers Landing, Tennessee
November 1866

Dead-Eye and Job reached the riverside sawmill of Elias Caruthers shortly after noon. They found a little, one-room shack at the edge of the bank about the size of a two-seat outhouse and a small dock that extended twenty feet or so at the water's edge. Or, rather, *blood's* edge. It was difficult to reconsider the terms of the Mississippi... to judge it the way it was now from how it had been before, constant and dependable.

There was a sign on the shack wall that read ELIAS CARUTHERS / SAWMILL & FERRY. RING BELL FOR SERVICE. Job dismounted and, taking hold of the rope, gave it a couple of pulls. The brass supper bell mounted atop the roof's ridge beam rang loudly, like a call to preaching on Sunday morning.

Soon, an old, gray-bearded man came walking down from the shelter of a sawmill a hundred yards away. He seemed in no big hurry, as though he'd rather put as much space between him and the tainted river as humanly possible.

"Howdy!" greeted the man. He looked on the verge of shaking hands, but refrained from the gesture. The elderly man appraised the two—one of a color his sons had fought to keep in chains and the other looking like Death warmed over—and decided to dispense with the socializing. "You folks wanting to cross? Don't appear to me you came looking to buy lumber or railroad ties."

"We are, indeed. Wayward travelers in need of your assistance," said the black man with a precious metal grin.

"What's over yonder?" Dead-Eye asked, studying the opposite bank. "Arkansas?"

"Missouri," Caruthers told him. "Arkansas is further down Memphis-way."

"What's your fee?"

"Ten cent a head if'n you have two legs. Fifteen for four-legged passengers."

"A mite pricey for a ferry ride, I'd say," mused the gunfighter.

"Had to increase my profit due to the effort," the ferryman spoke plainly. "Where it once took four men to oar across, now it takes eight. The river is twice as thick and three times more treacherous. Much more difficult to navigate since that unholy bitch in the black shroud did her deed."

Job's eyebrows rose to his hat brim. "You do say? Tell us about it."

"They showed up here around noon, two days ago. Three riders and a woman driving two black horses pulling an equally black wagon. The trio was a rough bunch; fresh out of the foulest of prisons… or the vilest pits of Hell. At least that was my impression. The woman was of Negroid blood, same as you. They had an extra mount with them… saddled, like it was ready and waiting for a rider to just happen along."

"And you took them across?"

"I did. Me and my sons. They paid their coin and we began the journey over." The old man frowned. "I'll not deny it… I began to think better of it halfway there. The five had an air about them that unsettled me."

"Five?" asked Dead-Eye. "I thought you said only four."

"The woman had a child on the seat next to her. A boy. Tall for his age, dark of hair and countenance. There was a sadness about him that made me wonder if he was there of his own accord."

The gunslinger looked over at Job. The mojo man's eyes narrowed and he nodded.

"There was something else," said Caruthers. "I had an awful feeling someone was in the back of the wagon. Maybe living… maybe not. My boys felt that, too, although we saw nothing to suggest such."

Job rummaged through a pocket of his vest and placed fifty cents in coins into the ferryman's leathery palm. Elias Caruthers whistled shrilly betwixt his tobacco-stained teeth. Eight strapping young men—four who looked unflatteringly like their papa—abandoned their work at the sawmill and ran down the hill to the ferry station.

"And, so, you took them to the other side?" Job continued.

"We did and was damned pleased to be rid of them! We left them on the bank and were halfway home, when the current grew peculiar beneath us. I've crossed this old river a thousand times or two, and I know every current and eddy in it. The boys cussed as they struggled with their oars and I was having a time of it keeping the rudder straight and true. I looked back over my shoulder and there was that woman in black, standing on the edge of the bank, with a book in her hand."

A dark expression crossed Job's face. "A book you say. Of what sort?"

"Well, it sure as hell wasn't the Holy Word, that's for certain! She opened that accursed tome and began to speak from it, waving her hand across the water; up and down, back and forth. It grew harder to pull the boat toward shore and, all of a sudden, there was no longer water in the Ol' Mississip. Blood, thick and crimson, coursed beneath us. It clotted and grew heavy on the oars' paddles and nearly sucked them down into its depths, with the fellers still hanging on for dear life. We finally made it across and back onto the safety of the dock. And there she was, standing yonder, laughing to bust a gut. If there was humor to her conjuring, we were the ones who were the butt of it."

As Dead-Eye and Job led the black Morgan and white mule—Brimstone and Balaam by name—onto the platform of the flatboat, the eight men grabbed twelve-foot oars that leaned against the far wall of the shed and took their places along the railing of the vessel, four on one side and four on the other. A moment later, they pushed away from the dock and headed westward across the surging channel of blood. The eight heaved and struggled with their oars, breaking a sweat, despite the chill of the winter's day.

"Why do you think she performed such an atrocity?" the black man wondered aloud. "Defiling the river the way she did?"

"Out of pure spite and cruelty, if'n you ask me," answered Caruthers. "Just so she could make sport of our misfortune. And misfortune it's been ever since!" He pulled a bandana up over his lower face and grimaced distastefully. "Like wading through the dregs of a slaughterhouse, it is!"

"Could have been another motive she had in mind for doing so," said Job.

"Like a warning, perhaps?" figured Dead-Eye. He could see by the expression on the mojo man's face that he was of the same mind.

As the boat inched its way toward the far bank, Dead-Eye shook his head. "It does stink to the high heavens, I'll allow that."

"Could be that some of that malodorous offense is coming from you as well," Job told his traveling companion. "Have you taken a lingering sniff of yourself lately? Even a buzzard would be hard up and desperate to give you a second glance."

Dead-Eye felt something wiggle through the bristles of his mustache and brushed it away with a pale finger. Maggots dropped to the boards of the flatboat. The gunfighter promptly mashed them beneath the heel of his boot. "I have become a mite ripe as of late. But, not nearly as much as I suspected. Figured by now that I'd be swollen up and stiffer than a rooster's cock in a henhouse. But it's not been that way a'tall."

"It's the hoodoo I've cast upon you," Job explained. "Ain't gonna do us a damn bit of good if you start putrefying and falling apart with our quest scarcely started. You're blessed by a spell of preservation. You may decay a bit and stink like a skunk atop a shit pile, but you'll remain whole until justice is dealt and Holland and his marauders receive their comeuppance. After that, well… you know, ashes to ashes, and dust to dust."

The cadaverous gunfighter grunted in response. "That's a mighty comforting way of putting it."

"I am not a mincer of words. You should well know that by now."

Soon, there was no more than two hundred feet between the boat and dry land. The animals reacted to the boat ride differently. Balaam was skittish at the sights and smells about him, eager to place his silver shoes upon the dust of the earth. Brimstone, on the other hand, seemed to find pleasure in the passage. He stuck his dark neck over the side railing of the flatboat and drank of the crimson flow until his belly was full. Then he stood proudly upon the bow, as if he were boating across the fetid channel of the River Styx itself… almost as though out of intimate recollection.

When, the boat reached the opposite shore and the ramp was dropped, the two travelers and their mounts disembarked. Job noticed that Elias was scowling back the way they had come, as though dreading the trip across the torrid tributary of gore.

"You performed a fine service bringing us across," the wiry negro told him. "True, you were paid for your effort, but I'm a-thinking you and your kin are deserving of something more."

The ferryman arched a bushy brow, intrigued. "And what would that be?"

"Y'all head back over to Tennessee and I'll see if I can't conjure a proper reward."

Old Man Caruthers looked at the young men aboard the ferry and shrugged.

Then, with groans of exertion and the flexing of work-hardened muscle, the crew began to propel the boat back into the sanguine currents of America's longest and mightiest waterway.

When they were a fourth of the way there, Job cupped his hands and hollered. "Tell me something! Which way did those scoundrels head?"

"Westward up that road behind you," the ferryman shouted. "There's a fork a couple of miles further. One heads toward Arkansas… the other into the high country of the Ozarks. Which direction they took when they got there, you'll have to figure that out for yourself."

Dead-Eye studied the mojo man with curiosity. "Reward, huh? Exactly what have you got in mind, witch doctor?"

Job glared at him, but didn't lambast him for using a term he found offensive and belittling of his chosen profession. He stood on the bank for a long moment, watching as the ferryman and his polemen struggled to make it across. Then, silently, he walked to Balaam and opened the flap of one of the mule's canvas packs. His dark hands dug around for a while, then grabbed hold of something and drew it from the depths.

It was a narrow cane of strange design, perhaps five feet in length from top end to bottom.

Dead-Eye appraised the walking stick. It was long and lean, the bottom half knotted, gnarled, and weathered gray in color, while the upper was of polished hickory with the carved head of a serpent at the very top. "What in tarnation do you have there?"

Job frowned, as if dreading the answer he was forced to give. "It's... um... a staff."

"I can see that, but..."

Irritated, the old man shook his head and then blurted it out. "Well, if you must know, it's the Staff of Moses!"

The gunfighter stared at him skeptically. "You're shitting me. *The* Staff of Moses? The one that brought the plagues down upon the heads of the Egyptians and parted the Red Sea?"

"That's right."

"And where would one acquire such a thing?"

Job held the staff proudly. "Won it in a poker game in Mobile, Alabama. The most Royal of Flushes claimed it fair and square, and not by deceit or trickery neither!"

"I suppose the feller who lost it just happened to have it stashed in his vest pocket for safekeeping?"

"He was a traveling preacher man who'd fallen to drink and degradation," explained the mojo man. "He was no longer worthy of such a sacred antiquity, so I relieved it from his possession... along with thirty-three dollars and the big railroad timepiece I tote in my vest."

Dead-Eye's good eye narrowed in scrutiny. "I've seen a few paintings of Moses in my time, but never toting a fancy snake-head cane."

"Truth be told, only the bottom half is the honest-to-goodness artifact. The top piece I had carved by a wood-working man in Birmingham."

"What do you aim to do with it?"

"You're about as dense as a tree stump," Job told him. "I'm aiming to break the hex Evangeline cast upon these waters."

"Think you can do it?"

"Never had the cause or opportunity to try it before." The mojo man approached the water's edge and stood there, contemplating.

Dead-Eye smirked. "Reckon you oughta light up a burning bush and ask Him for permission first?"

If Job's eyes could have cast fire, the gunslinger would've been a cinder in an instant. "Shameful of you, blaspheming in such a callous manner. Remember, your soul is stuck between Heaven and Hell. It can end up either way, so I'd shut those cold, dead lips of yours if I were you."

Dead-Eye scowled, but said nothing more. He simply watched as Job stepped off dry land and stood, ankle-deep, in the churning river of blood.

The negro removed his hat and held it reverently to his chest. Then he lifted his face to the sky. "Lord, I'm a-hoping you'll be helping me with this a mite, cause I'm a long ways from being a holy man and lacking the time to search out one of genuine faith and conviction." Then he stretched out his arm and slowly lowered the tip of the staff into the crimson current.

He stood there like that for a long moment, but nothing happened.

"Still as red as a visit from Aunt Ruby at the ill-tempered time of the month," mused the zombie.

"Hush up," hissed Job. "It's a big-ass river. Gonna take some doing."

Perplexed, he studied the channel of blood. Then a grin split his dark face. "Take yourself a look over yonder."

Dead-Eye looked across the river to the opposite bank where the ferry dock extended from the shore. The water there was no longer red, but rather its customary muddy brown. The Southerner watched as the crimson receded at an increasing rate. He shifted his gaze to the staff in Job's hands. Half the rod was dark with blood, as though it was absorbing the offending substance.

Job seemed to notice the rate of the water's transformation as well. He bore his weight upon the staff, imbedding it firmly into the silt and sand of the riverbed, then stepped spryly away. If the rising blood reached his hands while he was still gripping the stick, he was afraid it might enter his fingers and arms, and there was no telling what might happen to him then. Probably something irreversible and fatal.

Together, they stood on the Missouri bank and watched as the crimson continued to separate from the brown current, gravitating westward, as the staff siphoned the offensive ichor away from the channel of the Mississippi. Before long, the last trickles of scarlet were devoured by the staff and everything was as it should be. A loud cheer sounded from across the river and they looked to the far side. Elias Caruthers whooped and hollered with a big grin on his whiskered face, waving his hat joyfully in the air. In response, Job removed his own gray derby and took a humble bow.

A moment later, the stain of blood had evaporated from the length of righteous wood and it stood tall in the current in the same state as it had been before. Job yanked it from the riverbed and walked back over to the white mule.

"Never would've believed it if I hadn't seen it with my own eye," said Dead-Eye. His deep, tomb-hollow voice held an underlying mixture of admiration and awe. "A purveyor of voodoo and black magic implementing tools of divinity and holiness in such a way. Sinner and saint rolled into one."

"A helluva lot more sinner than saint," said Job in dismissal. "But I use the means I have at hand at the time." He slid the staff back into the belly of the canvas bag and tied the flap in place. "I reckon we'd best head out… try to whittle down as many miles between us and our prey as possible."

The gunslinger flashed a crooked grin. "Oh, is that what they are? Our unfortunate quarry? Pardon me, but from everything we've seen since leaving that clearing where I died back in Tennessee, and even before, they seem a far piece from being poor souls deserving of mercy."

"Not saying that a'tall." Job swung atop Balaam as his partner mounted Brimstone. "Just proclaiming our worth as adversaries. We're two to be reckoned with, so they'd best watch their wicked asses."

They looked toward the dirt trail that awaited them. In the gloom and shadow of the encroaching forest, it seemed ominous and unwelcoming.

Then, having nothing further to say on the matter, the two spurred their mounts and headed westward.

Chapter Three

Near Eminence, Missouri, West of the Mississippi
November 1866

When they reached the fork in the road, there was no denying which direction they should go.

A sign had been left to guide them. Not made by man, but *of* man.

From the looks of him, he had been a farmer—tall and rawboned, perhaps thirty years in age. He had been secured to a black oak tree with railroad spikes. One had been planted in the center of his forehead, one just beneath his breastbone, and one in his lower abdomen, just above his groin. He was a good four feet off the ground, so they figured the big one named Boar had hefted him up, while Rooster, that scrawny fellow with the skin deformity, had driven the spikes through him, into the tree, with a sledgehammer or some such implement. It looked as though he had been put there a couple of days ago. Buzzards had clawed away the flannel shirt that covered his chest and shoulders, picking and pulling until the meat and bone were revealed. One particularly vicious fowl had stripped away most of the scalp from the crown of his head. The flesh lay in tatters across his nose and down his ears. The man's eyes were gone. All that remained were glistening black holes.

The farmer's right arm had been trussed up and the index finger of his hand pointed skyward. In the center of his palm was carved the word HEAVEN. The boot on his right foot had been shucked off. The big toe of the exposed foot pointed toward the earth. HELL had been written across the arch with the point of a knife. The left arm was tied to a tree limb with rawhide leather. It pointed directly toward the road headed northwestward. The sleeve had been cut away and on the inner flesh of the forearm was scrawled the word CATASTROPHE.

"Cocky sons of bitches, ain't they?" remarked Dead-Eye.

"Unfortunately for this poor soul, yes," said Job. They regarded a long wagon parked at the side of the southwestern trail. A brace of mules were still tethered to its iron tongue. The bed was stacked high with wooden posts and barbed wire for fencing. Sitting on the seat were parcels that had been ripped open and their contents scattered across the roadway. A woman's calico dress and a china doll with silky golden hair. Its white face peered emotionlessly at them, the porcelain cracked and robbed of its flawless beauty. It was plain to see that the farmer had been on his way home from town, bearing supplies for labor and gifts for his loved ones.

"The waste of a man's life, just to leave a warning for the two of us." The zombie shook his head. "Such disregard sticks in my craw."

"Another reason why our quest must succeed," the mojo man told him. "Not only to retrieve the boy and punish his captors for the atrocities they've committed, but to prevent them from perpetuating even more cruelty."

They stared at the dead farmer for a moment more. "Well, it ain't fitting to leave him there. We'd best get him down."

"I agree… since we were partially to blame for his death."

The two men dismounted and went to work. Attempting to pry the man from the iron spikes was a difficult and unpleasant task. Once the remains were away from the tree and lying in the roadway, they found a shovel and pick in the back of the farm wagon. They buried the man in a grove of dogwood trees. The spot was drab and dismal on the cusp of winter, but would be a pleasant resting place come springtime with the budding of white blossoms and a blanket of new clover and daffodils. Knowing little else to do, they unhitched the mules and left the wagon parked where it was. While the two animals munched at dead grass by the roadside, Job set the shattered china doll on the wooden seat and pinned a note to the toy, telling the whereabouts of the ill-fated husband and father. He refrained from providing the lurid details of how he had met his demise or the sorry manner in which his body had been discovered.

They mounted Brimstone and Balaam and turned toward the left-hand trail. Where the other descended into the vast pastureland of Arkansas, this one rose gradually into the foothills of the Ozark Mountains.

"Catastrophe awaits us," said Dead-Eye. His pale hand—devoid of warmth or the pink of true life—absently caressed the ivory handle of the Dragoon pistol angled across his belly.

"Indeed, it does." Job dug his heels into the mule's sides, urging him toward the mountain trail.

The gunfighter's coal-black Morgan followed, but through no prompting on his master's part. Brimstone's eyes flared a muted red in his skull, like the sleeping embers of a fire eager to leap into flame once again. The animal it had once been may have balked at what awaited them, but the entity that now possessed it—who had endured eons of hellfire and damnation in the past—was anxious to assist his rider in dealing out a generous share of both to the band of marauders who had traveled the trail before them.

After several hours riding, they found themselves entering the high country. The trail became less traveled road and more of a narrow deer path. It was barely wide enough for a wagon, but it had served that purpose, for the tall, dead grass on either side had been trampled and flattened by the wheels of such a vehicle. It was safe to assume that it was the black cabin wagon drawn by the two equally dark horses that the witch drove. They began to suspect that the wagon's team—as well as the other horses that accompanied them—were of the same netherworldly state as Brimstone. Several times they found horse droppings—as ebony as charcoal—that lay upon the ground, still smoldering with heat, even days afterward.

As the land ascended and grew plentiful with boulders and heavy thicket, it began to snow. It came as only flurries at first, but a gradual drop in temperature and the dense, gray clouds overhead held the promise of greater accumulation. Job stopped long enough to pull a heavy coat from the mule's pack. He gathered it around his slight frame like a bale of cotton wrapped around a chicken bone.

Dead-Eye frowned. "Now if that ain't the ugliest damn garment I've ever laid eyes on, I don't know what is."

"Don't you be disrespecting my coat now!" snapped the mojo man. "Made it myself, with my own two hands."

"It's *what* it's constructed of that's got me bumfuzzled. It's like Joseph's coat of colors, but with hides instead."

"You are correct. It's sewn of the pelts of many critters. Red fox, grey fox, possum, coon, bobcat, groundhog, beaver, badger, skunk, squirrel… there's even a Siamese cat in there, if you take a closer look. Smells a mite gamey, but it's as warm as a whore's bed on a summer night." He took a pair of fuzzy, fur muffs and slid them over his ears. "Made these here out of mole pelts."

"You mean to tell me you dug a couple of moles from their hill, just to warm those pie-plates of yours?"

"I did," he admitted with pride. "Better they be on my ears than digging up some poor widow's garden. I can wrangle up a couple and make you pair, if'n you want."

"Much obliged, but no thanks." The snowfall began to thicken, and ice began to settle on the gunfighter's shoulders and hat brim. "If you have no heat left in your body to preserve, a garment or two more against the cold doesn't make a hell of a lot of difference."

As day bled into dusk, the trail grew harder and harder to distinguish in the gloom. They found refuge in a cave in the side of a bluff, one big enough to hold both them and the animals. While the wind picked up speed and howled mournfully around the entrance, they built a small fire with old newspapers and some whittling pieces of soft pine Job found in his pack. Luckily, the smoke drifted up through cracks in the rock overhead and didn't gather to smother them. Of course, Dead-Eye could have slept in a blast furnace in the middle of a forest fire and it wouldn't have bothered him none.

A couple of hours passed. Job partook of a supper of hardtack and beans, chasing the grub down with the bitter-strong, tar-black coffee he was so adept at brewing. Afterward, he smoked his pipe and stared sullenly into the flames.

After a while, Dead-Eye could stand the silence no longer. "You're beginning to get on my damn nerves, you know that?"

Job looked puzzled. "How come? I haven't said a word."

"That's the problem. You haven't been able to shut your mouth for three hundred miles and now your jaws are tighter than a tick on a hound's ass."

The mojo man simply nodded. He drew a lungful of pipe smoke, then released it through his nostrils with a long, shuddering sigh.

"So," said Dead-Eye. He eyed his companion closely, knowing it was time. "Evangeline."

"Yes." Job set his pipe aside and took a small tin flask from his hip pocket. The little man unscrewed the container and took a deep swallow of rye whiskey from within. He resembled a troubled man on the verge of confession—guilty, fearful, and angered by the circumstances that had brought him to that point in time. "But if I tell this story, I'll tell it from the beginning. And it'll be the very last time it'll grace anyone's ears, living or dead."

Dead-Eye nodded respectfully. "Agreed."

The little mojo man sighed deeply, then began. "I was born in Bogalusa Parish, deep in the swamplands of east Louisiana," Job began. "My papa was a practitioner of the voodoo arts from one of the southern islands down off in the Atlantic... Haiti or the Dominican. He was a tall man and as black as pitch, but he was of questionable character and motive. Spent far too much time drinking and whoring than taking care of his family in the manner that he should. My mama was a runaway slave. Escaped from a sugar plantation near Baton Rouge and hid away back in the darkest of swamps, taking up residence in places that no man of your color would dare set foot in. She'd been taught things by her mama before her, skills that were of value to folks in those parts. She was a soothsayer and concocter of bayou medicine—balms and potions made from cypress root, hanging moss, and the yolks of unborn gators. When she met Papa, it was lust at first sight. Not sure if they ever married properly, but they plowed that bed, from post to post, like two mules anxious to get the work done and get back to the barn. They had ten young'uns in all. I was the seventh son, just as my father was in his brood. Some say that gives a child a talent for certain areas of expertise, dealing in occult practices or the gift of healing. I never healed a hangnail or an ingrown toe, but I did have a knack for the dark arts.

"My father taught me the magic of his people and the deities they worshiped… Blanc Dani, Papa Legba, and the Grand Zombi. He also schooled me in devising and implementing the various gris-gris of my trade." Job absently raised a dark hand to the collection of charms that hung around his neck. "Mama taught me the things that her grandmother had passed on to her from the Dark Continent; practices such as the concocting of various potions and tonics, and divining for water and precious minerals. As I passed from a child into a young man, I grew masterful in my learning, as well as bold and prideful. It fretted my mother to no end, for she feared that I would grow up to be as atrocious and trifling as my papa.

"When I was seventeen, I was put off by a girl in the parish… a girl I had pursued to be my bride. In a rage, I cast a hoodoo upon her, causing her to grow a third breast betwixt the other two. It was a mean and spiteful thing to do. It grieved the poor girl so much that I soon regretted my dark deed and reversed the spell. I told myself from that day forward that my magic would only be used for the good of mankind and the detriment of evil. This placed contempt between me and my father. He saw me as weak and wasteful of the potential he had blessed me with. A year or so later, Papa was coming home from a drunken binge, when he disappeared in the bayou. Some say he stepped into a quicksand pool and was swallowed up. Others say that giant swamp spiders—the dreaded *La Sanguinaire*— dropped down from the trees and took him. Or, that he was eaten by Ma Gator, who measures eighteen feet from her snout to the tip of her tail. The only thing that was found of him was his mojo book, lying on the bank of the marsh. It is the same book that I carry with me to this day.

"I left my mother's house and set out to live my life, dependent upon no one, and ply my trade. The people of Bogalusa Parish didn't cotton much to my choice of profession and the unsavory aspects of it, but they were respectful and caused me no trouble. I soon caught the eye of a dark-haired, dark-eyed Cajun girl named Rosemonde Theriot. In the French language, her family name meant 'gift from God', but she was far from it. She was a wild and wicked woman; a witch in every sense of the word, both in practices and personality. She could sweet-talk you with a tongue dipped in honey one moment, then strike with the fury of a viper the next. Rosemonde was a mistress of spellcasting and conjuring, and if you wanted someone to fall madly in love with you or cause them a world of misery and pain, she was the one to seek.

"We took up house together and a tempestuous bond was formed. Passion and poison mingled one with another. She begat me eight young'uns, each more rotten and no-account than the one before. The last one was the runt of the litter, a quiet and frail daughter that we named Evangeline. The child was born with a veil of flesh upon her face—a caulbearer such are called—thus she was blessed with a penchant for shining and the predicting of futures. She also had a peculiar talent for necromancy and could converse with and call forth the spirits of the dead. Many a time we would discover her playing in the parish cemetery, visiting from crypt to crypt, talking to those who dwelt there, and them talking back in mortal voices. She was a nervous and uneasy child at first, scared of the critters and shadowy places of the bayou, but by her twelfth year, she feared nothing or no one. Like her ma, she walked tall and with authority, aware of the gifts she possessed and her willingness with which to use them.

"Rosemonde took the girl beneath her wing and began to school her in black magic. My wife possessed a book; a horrid tome bound in human skin. On its yellowed pages were inscribed ancient spells and incantations that no man or woman of our world should ever have knowledge of. They began to toy with alternate realms... cracking open the seams of time and space, breaching doorways and congregating—even fornicating—with the entities listed in the pages of that accursed book. Baal, Lamashtu, Dakshina Kālikā, Apophis, Yog-Sothoth, Hades, Mymahthu, and countless others. Under her mother's tutorage, Evangeline grew more powerful and arrogant. She began to call forth demons and fiends to torment the residents of Bogalusa Parish. It wasn't long before Cajun and Creole, Catholic and sinner alike, dreaded the setting of the sun and the Hell the night would bring under Evangeline's vindictive orchestration.

"Finally, ashamed of the evil my family had wrought, I studied my papa's mojo book, gathering the dark weapons that I had vowed I would never resort to using. The Parish became a battleground. The forces of darkness and light clashed and, eventually, the evil spawn of Evangeline's conjuring scurried back to the realms from which they came, like whipped pups with their tails between their legs. During the conflict, Rosemonde was abducted by Asmodeus, a demon of carnal desire, to be enslaved as his wife. I recall doing all that was humanly—and inhumanly—possible to prevent the fate that my wife had brought upon herself, but there was no stopping it. When it was over, the Parish was safe. My daughter agreed to leave Bogalusa and torment it no more. She departed in the dark of a moonless night and, with her, she took the accursed opus bound in flesh… the Book of the Dead… Kitab al-Azif … *Necronomicon*, as it is sometimes called."

Job's face was troubled in the flickering glow of the campfire. "At first, I stayed put, telling myself it was best that I stayed there and protect the Parish from further harm. Maybe that was true in part, but I began to realize that some of my hesitancy in pursing Evangeline was out of fear and uncertainty. To tell the truth, I was mortified of my own child. I knew that the magic between the damnable covers of that horrible tome was far beyond my simple voodoo and the quiver of spells and incantations my little book held. So, I stayed at the Parish and cowered. It wasn't until the third year of the War Between the States that I received word that Evangeline was up to her old tricks again. She had taken up with a European fellow by the name of Jules Holland, a nobleman cursed with vampirism. Along with a band of demons she had conjured, Evangeline accompanied him on a reign of terror, moving across the north and south, bringing death and torment to anyone who got in their way.

"So, I bought Ol' Balaam from a man in town, gathered up all that his packs could carry, and set off to confront her. For nearly three years now I have searched. I finally caught up to them the night they brutally murdered you in that backwoods' clearing in Tennessee, but I refrained from engaging them myself. I knew, at that moment, that I must prepare further and even the odds somehow, if I were to stop those hellish marauders. After they left, I approached the clearing and stared down at your lifeless body." The mojo man lifted his eyes from the dancing flames and flashed a wry grin Dead-Eye's way. "I nearly buried your sorry carcass and hit the trail again. But then I saw that big Dragoon pistol lying on the ground next to you and I got me an idea."

"And Dead-Eye was born," said the zombie gunfighter. "Or reborn, depending on how you look at it."

"Yes," agreed Job, "indeed, he was. Now I have a passel of magic and an immortal gunman to bless my quest and bring it to fruition."

Dead-Eye regarded the little man. "I'd say I resent you for doing it, but I have a quest of my own. And more of a chance of accomplishing it than when I left Georgia."

As the tall Southerner stared morosely into the flames of the fire, Job sensed that his companion's thoughts were troubled. "You are thinking about that boy on the riverbank, aren't you? The one with the brand upon his face."

Silently, the dead man nodded. A name rasped from his lips, whole and unforgotten. "Garland Hughes."

"You know you're never going to cross paths with that feller, don't you?"

"Maybe," the dead man said. "But if I ever do, I'll know him when I see him. There can't be a helluva lot of Garlands around these days."

Job nodded. He was disturbed by his companion's dismal mood. "As for your own son, don't fret none. We'll get to Daniel before harm can befall him. I vow that we will."

Dead-Eye said nothing in reply. He simply sat there and didn't react, as though he hadn't heard the man at all, although he had and in no uncertain terms.

His left eye—wide, blind, and aglow with foxfire—blazed within the shadow of his hat brim. The other, gray, hard, and as cold as a stone, watched the flames in somber contemplation. As well as in anticipation of what was to come.

Chapter Four

The Ozark Mountains
Mid-November 1866

For the better part of a week, they rode the snowy trails of the Northern Ozarks, traveling from ridge to ridge, searching for signs of those they pursued. The early snowfall didn't help matters. Any horse tracks or wagon ruts had been covered over by several inches of snow and ice, so tracking was nearly impossible. Brimstone seemed to be their only chance at keeping on track and not becoming hopelessly lost in the frozen labyrinth of hills, hollows, and canyons. Being possessed of a demon himself, the black Morgan seemed to be able to sense others of his kind, in close proximity or even miles away. Given that Jules Holland's three henchmen—Snake, Boar, and Rooster—as well as the horses that accompanied them were of that hellish fraternity, he seemed honed in on their general direction.

One afternoon, they happened upon a man traveling on foot through a narrow pass. He journeyed eastward, while they continued to the west. He was a young man, perhaps in his early twenties, brawny in frame with copper-red hair and a thick, bristly beard of the same rusty hue. He was dressed in a warm buffalo coat, scarf, woolen britches, and heavy boots, and walked with the aid of a long cane of black wood that looked to be more root than an object fashioned from limb or trunk. His headgear was also a peculiar choice for the area and weather he traveled in—a tan bowler hat, similar to the one Job sported. He carried a heavy canvas pack across his broad back and hanging from a sling across one shoulder was a Purdey double-barrel shotgun of British make.

"Top of the morning to ye fine gentlemen!" he greeted as they met midway in the canyon. His voice possessed a bold, lilting Irish brogue. As they rode closer, they surmised that the redness of his checks and nose was more due to a love of strong drink than wintry weather.

"Howdy," replied Dead-Eye without much enthusiasm.

Job's nature was more neighborly. "Well, hello there, young man!" He studied the Irishman curiously. "You're the first friendly soul we've come across in the past few days. The *only* soul, to tell the truth."

"And you are the only two I've come across since evening last," he said with a smile. "The name's Dermot McAllister. Birthed and bred in County Cork of the beloved isle of Ireland, and a peddler of goods and services by trade. My specialty ranges from carpentry to blacksmithing, and I do admit I have a somewhat artistic hand when it comes to carving toys and play-pretties for the youngsters."

"What are you doing on foot, out in the middle of nowhere, in this sort of weather?" asked Dead-Eye. "And with no horse beneath you?"

"I prefer to earn my living peddling in the mountains of this great land," McAllister told him. "The Ozarks, Rockies, Appalachians... I've spent the last five years walking the length and breadth of their majesty. The people of the high country are in need of the wares and services I offer, so I fare well in these remote territories. If they have no coin to part with, I barter. A meal or a night's stay beneath a dry roof... or strong libation if it's available. Whiskey, wine, or homebrewed moonshine... it is my vice in life, I do declare." The Irishman eyed the black Morgan admiringly. "As for horses, they are lovely and magnificent creatures, but you'll not find me atop one's back. The last thing, other than me own legs, which carried my weight was the ship that brought me across the sea to your bountiful country and that was a mortifying ordeal indeed. This fine animal... Begorrah, he is a stunning one to behold! If you will allow me the liberty, I shall commit his likeness to memory and, someday, carve a likeness in wood for some deserving lad or lass."

Job regarded the burly young man, who stood there, looking as completely out of his element as anyone he had ever seen before. "Tell me, Mister McAllister... have you happened across three riders? Rough men of dastardly intent? And a young woman dressed in black, driving a black wagon?"

The expression of good humor on the peddler's robust face seemed to falter and he spat to the side in disgust. "Indeed, I have! A trio of scoundrels a few steps shy of Purgatory... or a few steps out of it, you might say. And the woman who drove the team of raven-black horses... she had the look of an enchantress about her, and not in a favorable manner. The sort of lass that would cause the dreaded *Dearg Due* to give sway."

"Was there a young'un with her?" asked Dead-Eye. "A boy?"

"Not that I saw. The wagon had a cabin, so if there was such a lad, he may have been inside. It was an intolerable day... bitter cold and full of bluster."

"Did you have words with these travelers?" Job asked.

McAllister laughed with contempt. "If I had, I'd likely not be standing here before you. They were the type you choose to ignore and feel blessed if they ignore you in return. To tell the truth, I watched them from the window of an eating establishment as I feasted upon beer, possum stew, and sourdough. There was a blazing hearth not six feet away, yet the sight of the four and their creatures chilled me to the very marrow."

"Where did this sighting take place?"

"At Blood Moon Ridge, twelve miles southwest of here, past the Missouri line and into the Arkansas stretch of the mountains. Just a wee village inhabited by poor hill folk, ignorant in book learning, but savvy in the ways of the wilderness." He looked from the little black man to the tall Southerner with the blind eye and hogleg pistol holstered across his belly. He granted them an expression of warning. "I'd ride clear of that settlement if I were you. They're a surly and inhospitable bunch. Not sure if they'd take kindly to either of you. A man of color or a dandified gunfighter. They boast a pistolero themselves... a nasty and despicable charlatan by the name of Coltrane."

Dead-Eye's good eye narrowed. "Sounds like a man aching to be tried."

"Don't be getting any notions," Job warned him. "If we go, we'll go peaceably."

"My advice is to not go at all," the Irishman suggested. "There's a dark secret about the place. A foreboding. I knew of such places back in sweet Erin. Places said to be inhabited by banshees and *taibhse*."

"So did I, in the bayous of Louisiana," said the negro. "But neither of us are strangers to evil territory nor the ones who dwell there. We're obliged for your concern, nevertheless."

Before departing company, Job and the peddler did a bit of friendly haggling. The mojo man came away with tobacco, sulfur matches, gunpowder, percussion caps, and a brass bullet press gaged for a .36-caliber, the same as his pepperbox pistol. In return, McAllister gained half a bottle of scotch from Job's pack and several voodoo charms; a protection *garde* consisting of an alligator tooth soaked in herbs and sealed in a small bottle, or *mavangou*, as well as a *juju* made from the dried nutsack of a wild boar and filled with garlic, goat weed, chicken feathers, and ground tortoise shell for good health and prosperity.

As the Irishman prepared to head out, Dead-Eye regarded him skeptically. "You'd fare much better on horseback. It's gonna be a damn cold night. You're liable to ice over before morning."

"Aye," said the peddler. "One of these days, I'm liable to down a snootful of rotgut and head into the mountains somewhere and freeze to death. If so, me ghost shall roam the hills and hollows until it finds contentment and peace. But not tonight. I've got this buffalo hide and the scotch to warm my cantankerous bones. Now, if you fine gentleman will pardon me, I'll be on my way."

The two riders watched as the young peddler walked a distance down the canyon, heading due east. Suddenly, he stopped and turned on his heels. His cheerful demeanor was dampened by concern and, perhaps, fear. "There be a full moon out tonight," he told them.

"Yes," answered Job with a nod, for he was aware of the lunar cycle and its passing. "Most certainly."

"Take heed," Dermot McAllister advised. "There be beasties about."

As the man continued onward down the trail, Dead-Eye shook his head. "What'd he mean by that?"

Job shrugged his narrow shoulders, but his eyes were grim. "Can't likely say. But we'd best be on guard, just in case."

Together, they reined their mounts westward, aware that there was a long stretch ahead of them before they reached Blood Moon Ridge.

That night, they camped in a clearing amid a stand of tall pines and blue spruce. The bitter wind that had blown almost constantly during their time in the Ozarks was strangely absent. The sky was clear and, just as Dermot McAllister had said, there was a full moon as yellow as newly-churned butter high in a starless sky.

After supper and a leisurely smoke of his pipe, Job nestled beneath woolen blankets and his coat of many pelts and fell asleep. Brimstone and Balaam were tethered a few yards away, quiet and weary from a long day of toting their masters.

Being deceased, Dead-Eye required no sleep, but found himself nodding off, as he did from time to time. As he sat with his back to the trunk of a maple tree, he dreamt of happier times, when he had been the one named Joshua Wingade... before the War had corrupted his spirit and the vampire Jules Holland had stolen his family. Pleasant thoughts occupied his mind. Hunting deer and coon with his father as a young man, and family outings and quiet evenings beside the hearth with his wife, Elizabeth, and son, Daniel.

From there, the dreams descended into nightmare. The wanton killing and endless death and hardship of the Civil War. The long stretch of torture and misery at the Northern prison camp. Then returning home only to find that the love of his life had been violated and damned to the life of the *Nosferatu*, and that his only child was abducted by those responsible. The horrors he had encountered during his pursuit of the outlaws followed, ending with his last moments as a living man…

"Daniel! I will come for you! I promise!"

Dead-Eye awoke, startled.

Something wasn't right. He could sense it. He heard soft, restless noises coming from the animals at the edge of the clearing. The mule was skittish… while the black Morgan was stark still and on guard. In the darkness, Dead-Eye saw the horse's eyes glow crimson, like the tip of a hot poker, and, when he snorted, heat and cinder were expelled.

"Brimstone," he whispered. "What is it, boy?"

Nearby, something howled. Not a dog. Something much bigger and much more fierce in nature. The sound rose skyward, echoing off canyon walls, sweeping through the naked branches of leafless trees. It was a guttural, bestial sound etched with savagery and brutal intent.

Dead-Eye drew his revolver and cocked the hammer.

"What was that?" exclaimed Job, popping up out of the warm folds of his blankets like a child's jack-in-the-box.

The creature howled again. Louder. Closer.

The gunfighter's good eye narrowed. The blind eye cast a pale glow upon the snowy ground of the clearing. "Company's coming."

They listened. Something big and full of fury was tearing its way through the underbrush from the west. Brimstone tossed his head and snorted, tugging at the leather reins that were tied to the trunk of a leafless sycamore. Balaam did the same. His pink eyes were bright and wild with fright.

Dead-Eye aimed and snapped off two shots, parting the animals' tethers, freeing them.

Job rolled out of his bedroll and stood in his stocking feet next to the campfire. He had drawn a long-bladed knife from a sheath within the left sleeve of his shirt. His pepperbox laid across the brim of his derby hat, six feet from reach.

Abruptly, the beast tore out of the thicket and landed on two feet at the edge of the clearing. Dead-Eye and Job had to study it for a moment to figure out exactly what it was. One thing was for certain, it was aiming to do some damage and wasn't particular about who the first victim might be.

Initially, they thought it was a wolf. Its massive head was canine in nature, the snout elongated, the ears long and pointed, and its fangs were sharp and dripping with thick slaver. Its eyes were dark but belied an intelligence that was more human than animal. It was the brute's body that told them that it was much more than a wolf. It possessed the long, muscular arms and legs of a man, and stood like one, rising a good eight feet in height. It possessed a thick coat of coarse brown hair, from head to foot, and its shoulders were as broad and strong as that of a Brahman bull. The fingers of its hands were long and tipped with sharp claws. There was no denying that they could rip flesh asunder with little effort, as easily as fingernails through scant cobwebs.

"What is that thing?" asked Dead-Eye.

"I don't rightly know," said Job. "Never seen the likes of its kind before."

The zombie raised his sidearm and aimed squarely at the monster's chest.

"Whatever the critter is, it's a dead one now." The Dragoon boomed twice, filling the night air with powder flash and smoke.

Two large wounds opened up in the center of the beast's broad chest. The impact rocked the wolf back on its heels, but it failed to collapse. It looked down at the bullet holes and a deep staccato of a growl rumbled up out of its gullet.

"Is that son of a bitch *laughing* at me?"

"I reckon so. Look!"

The .44-caliber holes in the creature's chest spouted blood for a second, then expelled the lead balls and slowly began to heal up. Soon, the flesh and hair had grown back over and there was no sign that the damage had ever been done.

"Well, shitfire." The words were scarcely out of Dead-Eye's mouth, when the wolf was across the clearing and upon him. Its massive weight drove him to his back in the snow. He touched off another round, sending it through the creature's snout and into its nasal cavity. The thing unleased a bloody sneeze, sending the lump of lead back at him. Then the claws of its right hand raked across his torso, from collarbone to the bottom of his ribcage. The nails slashed open the silk of his shirt and parted dead flesh and muscle, grating against the flats of his rib bones.

Suddenly, the gunslinger felt the creature's weight lift away. Past the thing's hirsute shoulder, Dead-Eye saw Brimstone. The black horse had the scruff of the fiend's neck in his teeth, tossing the critter aside as if it were no more than a puppy. It landed on its back in a snowdrift, then rose to its feet with an angry growl. It took a vicious swipe at the horse, but Brimstone was quicker. It caught the thing's wrist between its jaws and bit down. The clawed hand was cleanly severed and dropped, twitching and flexing, to the ground.

Both men watched in fascination as the splintered bone and torn sinew of the stump swiftly began to knit together and grow another hand. In fact, at first it was clearly a man's hand, hairless and pink. Then brown fur sprouted and the short nails of the fingers grew from one inch to more than six.

Enraged, it launched itself onto Brimstone's back, taking the Morgan's pitch-black mane firmly in its hands. Its hairy legs clutched the flanks with its calves the way a human might. It dipped its wolfish head toward the horse's neck, intending to tear into it with jagged, yellowed fangs.

It didn't have a chance, however. Balaam unleased a *hee-haw*, reared on his back legs, and brought his front hooves down forcefully upon the creature's back. The white mule's silver hooves burrowed deep and traveled downward. At the same time, the wolf critter's hair singed and the skin and muscle underneath opened—blistering, spouting gray smoke and the stench of burnt flesh. Beyond the wound, its spine could be seen, exposed, from neck to tailbone. The creature shrieked and leapt to the ground. It stumbled and dropped to one knee, apparently overwhelmed with pain.

An expression crossed Job's face, as though something had suddenly dawned on him. "Silver!" he yelled at Dead-Eye. "Load with silver!" While the brute was still struggling to stand, the mojo man ran forward and sliced the tendons above the beast's heels, crippling him. There was no healing of sinew this time. The double wounds smoked and sizzled like strips of bacon on an iron skillet.

Screaming with a howl of anguish and torment, the critter fell to its side and rolled onto its back. Dead-Eye watched it warily as he opened his frock coat and revealed a sawed-off twelve-gauge scattergun that dangled from a leather sling underneath. He cracked the breech and fished two brass shotgun cartridges from his coat pocket. The projectiles that showed from the open ends were cast from sterling silver. He loaded the gun, closed the breech, and walked over to the creature.

The beast bared its long fangs and snarled in defiance. Viciously, he took a swipe at the gunfighter's legs. Dead-Eye stepped away swiftly, but the wolf's claws parted the cloth of one of his britches legs just below the kneecap. The one-eyed zombie grunted, vexed at the damage to his clothing, then unloaded both barrels into the critter's torso.

Job joined him as they stood and watched the hellish creature die. It lurched violently, its limbs twisting and contorting in agony. Then it grew rigid and became still. Slowly, the coarse brown hair fell away and the wolfish features of its face receded. In amazement, they witnessed the hellish fiend as it transformed into a man. The fellow was lean and rough of countenance, sporting shaggy brown hair and a beard. Soon, he lay naked, his hairless body showing no sign of the fatal injuries he had sustained moments before.

"*Well, I'll be damned,*" said Dead-Eye. "What the hell was he?"

"A lycanthrope," Job told him, "or a werewolf, as some folks call them. A changeling cursed by the bite of another. I don't rightly know how it comes about. It could be a tainting of the bloodline or something downright supernatural. I'd heard of such before, but this is the first time I've actually seen one in the flesh."

The gunfighter returned the shotgun to its place beneath his coat and eyed the knife in Job's hand. "Silver, huh?"

The mojo man nodded. "Bought it from a silversmith a while back, while I was first on the trail of Holland and his bunch. Figured it might come in handy. Glad I had the foresight to do so now."

Dead-Eye walked over and ran a gentle hand through the Morgan's black mane. "I'd say we have a posse of four, rather than two. Looks like Brimstone and Balaam can hold their own in a fight."

Job attended to the white mule as well. "I'll say. Formidable adversaries, for mortal man and devil alike."

"What do you figure we should do with this fella?"

"Let him lie where he is," said the negro. "Tomorrow, we'll wrap him in a horse blanket and tote him with us. See if someone further up the trail lays claim to him." He studied Dead-Eye's torn shirt and the exposed ribcage where the werewolf's claws had peeled away the lifeless flesh. "You want I should mend that for you?"

"It can wait till morning. I'll button my coat, so the frost doesn't get to my innards."

They tethered the animals back to the tree once again, then returned to the campfire. "You get yourself some shut-eye," the gunfighter suggested. "I'll stand watch the rest of the night."

Job nodded and returning the silver knife to the scabbard beneath his sleeve, climbed back into his blankets. "While you're at it, throw some more wood on the fire. And load up with silver. Your pistol and scattergun both. I'm hard-pressed to believe there's only one of these critters about. Could be a whole passel of them."

"Hopefully not all in a single night," Dead-Eye said. As his companion snuggled into his bedroll and was soon fast asleep, the lanky cadaver found some dry limbs to fortify the fire.

He thought of the human sign at the crossroad and what had been carved into the dead farmer's forearm. "Catastrophe for damn sure," he muttered.

Then he sat with his back to the maple once again and, taking paper cartridges and brass shells from his pocket, prepared his guns for the chance of further peril.

Chapter Five

Blood Moon Ridge
Mid-November 1866

As it turned out, the Irish peddler was right about the little mountaintop settlement of Blood Moon Ridge. It only consisted of a few ramshackle buildings gathered around a rutted, dirt road—a general store, an adjoining restaurant, a livery stable, and several weathered houses that looked on the verge of collapse, perched precariously on stone ledges. Heavy forest stretched to the north of the town, while the vast landscape of the Arkansas hill country, and the flatlands beyond, yawned to the south.

As they rode down the center of the slush-covered street, Dead-Eye and Job studied their surroundings. Snow lay thick and heavy across the bowed roofs of the structures, as well as around the porches and walls, a good two feet deep in places. There was the blackened, stone foundation of a burnt-out building between the store and the stable. Spying a charred podium at the very back, they figured it had once been a church. From the looks of it, it appeared that it had been that way for quite a while.

"Never known folks who lost a church who didn't do their level best to build it back again," said Job.

"Perhaps we're amongst heathens," said Dead-Eye with a thin grin of bloodless blue lips.

The mojo man looked over his shoulder to where the blanket-wrapped body was tied to Balaam's back. "Could be... or something a mite worse in nature."

They reined their mounts toward the boardwalk in front of the eating establishment. A fat-bellied man with a bushy white beard, decked out in threadbare overalls, left his bench, and stood. He stretched, then walked to the railing and stared at them.

"Got a dead man here for you to take a look at," Job told him.

The man shifted his eyes from the bundle on the mule to the tall, pale man astraddle the Morgan. "Which one?"

"Just step your lazy hillbilly ass down here and take a look-see, will you?" grated Dead-Eye with an edge to his voice.

As the man left the porch and sauntered over to the mule, the mojo man cut his eyes sharply to the side. "If you don't shut the hell up, these folks are liable to bullwhip, tar and feather, and hang us both. I know that'd be a minor inconvenience to you, but it would put a damper on my bright and cheerful temperament something awful."

The fellow with the white beard opened a flap of the horse blanket and jerked the corpse's head up by the hair of his head. He stared at the man's face and grunted. Shaking his head, he cupped his hands over his mouth and hollered. "Gabel! Get over here and take a look at this!"

They watched as a door of one of the houses opened and several men walked out. The one in the lead was tall and thin, with shaggy black hair down to his shoulders and a salt-and-pepper beard midway down his breastbone. He had a mean and trifling look to his deep-set eyes as he trudged down the street and approached the man beside the mule. When he got there, he jerked the dead man's head up and stared him flat in the face. "Arlo," he said, sending a spritz of tobacco juice through his uneven teeth, into the snow at the mule's feet. He looked up at the black man. "You the one who killed him?"

"I had a hand in it," admitted Job, "but he's the one who put him down for the count."

The man named Gabel turned and regarded Dead-Eye, as did the others in the group...eight of them in number and brothers from the keen resemblance to their leader. "Ain't pleasing to a man when someone guns down his kin in cold blood."

"Neither is it pleasing when some dadblamed fool turns into a critter and tries to eat you," the gunfighter replied.

Gabel eyed the big Colt jutting from Dead-Eye's holster. "Well... Arlo was a peculiar soul."

"Ain't you gonna ask why he's buck-ass naked?"

The long-haired man shrugged. "Like I said... he was peculiar." He turned to the other fellows. "Tote him on back to the house."

As Job and Dead-Eye swung down and tied their animals to a hitching post outside of the restaurant, they were aware that Gabel hadn't left with his relations. He continued to stand there and stare at them with that sly expression in his gray eyes. He didn't exactly seem mad or disturbed by

Arlo's death. And he didn't seem to be a threat; he didn't even carry a sidearm. It was like watching a fox sitting on top of a henhouse, wondering why he was up there, rather than inside the shed, doing what foxes were born to do.

Job thought it safe enough to ask the man a question. "A bunch rode through here a few days ago. Three fellows… maybe four… on horseback. Had a woman in black with them…"

"Driving a coal-black wagon." Gabel spat again. "Yeah, we seen 'em."

"Didn't kick up a ruckus or nothing?"

The lanky man smiled a little. "You might say we respected one another. We knew what they were, and they knew what we were in return."

"And what was that?" countered Dead-Eye. "Ignorant, lice-ridden ridge runners that stink like a privy full of freshly-laid turds?"

Job closed his eyes and wearily shook his head. "Remind me later to cast a spell of tact and discretion upon that renegade tongue of yours."

Gabel laughed. His eyes didn't match his burst of good humor, however. "Y'all going in for a bite to eat?"

"I reckon so," said the black man. "The sun's three hours high and I've got a hankering for vittles."

"Maybe I'll send a feller over to converse with you. Provide you with a little entertainment whilst you eat your breakfast." Gabel's grin turned into a leer. "Of course, everyone he's ever entertained is sleeping six feet under sod now."

The mountain man laughed, then turned and started back toward the ramshackle house.

"Come on," said Job. "Let's go inside, do our business, and be gone. This place is starting to sour both my stomach and my spirit."

The two entered the restaurant, which consisted of four tables, an eating and drinking counter, and a doorway that led to a kitchen. They could hear the sound of meat sizzling in a cast iron skillet somewhere in the back and the air was thick and pungent with the odor of grease.

They took a seat at a table at the front window, aware that the eyes of the patrons were upon them. A scraggly, young woman with hair the hue of corn silk, wearing a dress sewn from flour sacks, appeared and stood regarding them. The expression on her homely face was a cross between boredom and contempt.

"Sorry, but we ain't accustomed to serving nigg—"

Job's glare froze her tongue in mid-sentence. "Young lady, if that nasty word stings my ears, I'll curse you with a passel of ill-tempered young'uns with crossed eyes and webbed toes, screaming and squalling like a litter of bobcats from dusk till dawn."

The girl eyed the charms around the black man's neck and took pause. She knew of the granny women thereabouts and the mountain magic they were capable of. Could be that this fellow's magic was more potent and a sight more vindictive. She looked over at the tall, pale man with the blind, yellow eye. "You reckon he could do that?"

"If he had a mind to," Dead-Eye told her. "He's of a quarrelsome disposition this morning. I'd say he'd give you twelve, maybe fourteen, if you were to cross him."

She sighed, knowing better than to push her luck. "So, what're you having?'

"Whatcha got?"

"Squirrel, possum, muskrat, deer. If'n you don't cotton to wild game, we got hog. Ham, bacon, pork... you name it."

"Bring me a plate of eggs, chitlins, and mountain oysters, with a biscuit or two on the side. And buttermilk if you have it."

Dead-Eye regarded the little man. "So, when it comes to pig, you prefer to eat it from the inside out, do you?"

The mojo man nodded. "Guts, balls, and all."

While they waited, an elderly man in a battered, gray forage cap and woolen coat turned from the bar and regarded them. "Saw y'all ride in with a body slung over the ass of your mule. Who was it?"

"Some feller named Arlo," said Dead-Eye.

The old man shook his head. "Well, that sure ain't gonna set well with the Bruley Brothers, especially Gabel. Kin is like gold in the pocket to them, and you've done gone and picked it. They're bound to take offense and come for you. Or send someone to deal with you."

"We're not aiming to stick around that long," Job told him. "What lies beyond town, to the west of here?"

"Four miles down the trail is Blue Sky Meadow. Old Granny Marigold lives in a cabin thataways. Then eight miles further is Keyhole Pass that leads down off the mountains, into the bottomland. I'd bet a chaw of tobacco and a lucky buckeye you won't make it, though. Heavy snow is on the way, and it'll seal that pass up tighter than a spinster's cooch before morning. My ol' bones have been complaining something awful for the past couple of days. They're as true as a preacher's handshake."

Before long, the woman had brought Job his breakfast and he commenced to eating. Dead-Eye idly looked through the window and noticed folks ducking into buildings and making themselves scarce as someone walked down the center of the street.

"Looks like our entertainment is on the way."

"Well, if things get out of hand, have the courtesy to take it outside," Job told him, skewering a boiled testicle with the tines of his fork. "I don't aim to get gut-shot in the crossfire. Such a thing can ruin a man's appetite."

They heard heavy footfalls on the boardwalk outside. Then the door of the restaurant burst open and a man swaggered in like he owned the place, with a generous amount of acreage besides.

Job nodded toward the door, cutting a gold and silver grin. "The pistolero. Coltrane."

Dead-Eye grunted, regarding the man who approached them. "A couple feet shy of what I was expecting."

"Don't let that fool you none. A chipmunk is as cute as can be, but he can pert near bite your finger in half if he has a mind to."

Coltrane was dressed a bit differently than the others in the mountaintop burg of Blood Moon Ridge. He wore store-bought clothing, not handmade, as well as a long, tan slicker coat and high-peaked hat. He wore a fancy two-holstered gun belt of hand-tooled leather bearing two Colt Navy pistols strapped around his hips. He would have been a formidable-appearing opponent for sure, except for the fact that he was lacking in stature. In fact, he was a good six inches shorter than the wiry, little mojo man.

He crossed the floor and stood at their eating table for a long moment, appraising them from the shade of the big hat. When he finally spoke, his voice was trying hard to be masculine and intimidating. "I heard tell you two killed my brother Arlo."

"If Arlo was the bare-assed feller we toted in on my mule, I reckon we did," Job told him. He poured a puddle of buttermilk into a corner of his plate and began to sop it with a biscuit.

"Then I've come to settle the score with you," Coltrane declared. The fellow was much younger than Gabel Bruley and the others, with a rash of adolescent blisters upon his face and a bristly coating of peach fuzz across his upper lip.

"So, your mama let you loose from the teat long enough to strap on your guns and walk over here to pester us?" asked Dead-Eye. "What are you? Four foot?"

"Five two!" snapped Coltrane. "Now, we can do this here or on the street. It's up to you."

"Hold up a minute. I gotta size a man up before I face him in gun battle. I ain't accustomed to dealing with young'uns. What's your age? Twelve?"

Coltrane's face reddened. "Seventeen years!"

"And how many men have you killed?"

The young man puffed up like a bullfrog. "Twenty-four! Drilled and buried before they knew what hit 'em!"

"And you're aiming for me to be number twenty-five?"

Coltrane nodded toward Job, who ate his meal, seemingly unconcerned. "Yessir. And after you're laid out cold, I'll shoot this little nigg— "

Job leveled his fork at the stubby gunfighter. "You finish that sentiment, you sawed-off little runt, and I'll cast a hoodoo on you that'll whittle a dozen more inches off that frame of yours. You'll be able to walk beneath a cow and comb your hair with the udders."

"I'd take him at his word," the tall Southerner advised.

It was clear to see that the pair's remarks were rubbing the boy's ego raw in a few sensitive areas. "Enough talk! Here or outside?" His hands trembled at his sides, precariously near the holsters. He was aching to draw those pistols.

"I reckon we'd best take it outdoors," Dead-Eye told him. "Wouldn't want to disturb these folks none." As he left his chair, he regarded Job. "Looks like this will be my first honest-to-goodness showdown. You want to come out and watch?"

"I'll observe from the window," mumbled the black man, continuing to feed his face.

Soon, the two gunfighters stood in the icy slush and mud of the main street. Coltrane backed up until there was a good thirty feet between the two. On the porch of the old house stood Gabel Bruley and the rest of the brothers. They seemed anxious to see the tall man fall for what he had done to poor Arlo.

"As I ain't ever been in a proper gunfight before, you might have to coach me on its etiquette," said Dead-Eye. "I faced down a feller on a store porch once, but that didn't fare well for me. He died, but so did an old woman behind him and I got my neck stretched for my trouble."

"Liar! Ain't nobody survived a hanging before!" snapped Coltrane. He stood with his feet spread apart and his hands splayed over the curved handles of his .36-caliber revolvers.

Dead-Eye grinned. "You'd be surprised." He studied the little gunslinger with his one good eye. "You want I should fetch a milking stool for you to stand on whilst you shoot at me?"

"I'm sick of your damn mouth," snarled Coltrane. "Now, you'd best draw that big hog leg of your'n, cause I'm sure as hell gonna draw mine!" He eyed the tall man's pale hand. It hung, limp and unconcerned, at his right thigh, a good ways from the Colt Dragoon angled across the belly of his shirtfront.

"Let's get to it then." Dead-Eye looked over at Job, who watched through the panes of the restaurant, and shook his head, as if saying *what a dumb-ass.*

The one named Coltrane wasted no more time. He dipped his right hand swiftly, pulled the pistol smoothly, then cocked and squeezed the trigger. Abruptly, the gun in his grasp exploded. Twisted fragments of blued steel spun through the air, along with his thumb and two of his fingers.

"What the shit happened?" he screamed, staring down at the bloody stumps at the ends of his knuckles.

Dead-Eye stood there, holding the smoking Dragoon in his bony hand. "I put a bullet down your barrel." His gaunt face was as pale and emotionless as that of a dead man… because that was precisely what he was.

"Son of a bitch!" Coltrane ignored his mangled right hand, grabbing for the other Navy revolver with his left.

Before the boy could clear leather, Dead-Eye fanned the hammer of the forty-four, putting slugs through both of Coltrane's kneecaps. The little man dropped to his back in the street, screaming and bucking wildly.

By the time Gabel Bruley and the others reached their wounded brother, Job had finished his meal and was at the hitching post, untethering Balaam. Dead-Eye was doing the same with Brimstone.

Gabel's narrow face no longer held the crooked smile. His expression was as cold and final as the face of a tombstone. "It ain't fitting, you treating our kin in such a way."

"Wasn't fitting, you sending General Tom Thumb to stand toe to toe with the likes of me either," Dead-Eye told him flatly. If Gabel's expression was a tombstone, the gunfighter's was an entire graveyard. "Bury the one and tend to the other, and forget we ever rode through this sorry town."

Gabel grinned cruelly as they mounted their animals and rode westward along the single street of Blood Moon Ridge. His tobacco-stained teeth seemed slightly longer than they had before. "Y'all take care out there on the trail," he yelled at them. "There's a full moon tonight. Things get downright treacherous in these parts at this time of month." Then he laughed coarsely and walked back to the house to see to his wounded brother.

A few minutes later, they were away from the town and headed toward the western end of the ridge. Dark clouds gathered overhead, obstructing the sun and throwing a gray cast upon the mountain. A stiff wind blew through the leafless trees, as sharp as a razor. Job gathered his coat of pelts about him and hunkered in the saddle. "Tell me something."

Dead-Eye glanced over at his companion. "Yeah?"

"Was your pistol loaded with silver?"

The zombie in the black broadcloth suit nodded. "It was."

"Then that Coltrane feller wasn't the same as Arlo," he told him. "If so, those knee wounds would've smoked like a gambler's cheap cigar and he'd given up the ghost. Those silver slugs would've been pure poison to him."

"You think Gabel Bruley and the rest of his clan are of savage blood?"

Job nodded. "Did you study them any? All had their eyebrows grown together and their first fingers were longer than the middle one. True signs of a lycanthrope. So, more'n likely, we'll be running into them later tonight when that moon shows itself."

Dead-Eye laid his hand upon the ivory grip of the Dragoon. "Beasties."

Job said nothing more. They rode silently as the day grew colder, promising the bite of forthcoming winter and the hardship to come.

Chapter Six

Blue Sky Meadow
Mid-November 1866

"You reckon this is the old woman's place?" Dead-Eye asked as they exited a tall stand of evergreen and pine.

The forest gave way to a broad expanse of open land that crested the mountaintop. In the spring, it was likely covered with all manner of wildflowers and clover. That frigid November day, however, its earth was blanketed with six inches of newly-fallen snow. The trail split the place known as Blue Sky Meadow in half, with a small cabin of roughly-hewn logs on the right side and a ramshackle barn to the left. Other outbuildings stood scattered here and there—a chicken coop, a smokehouse for curing meat, and a privy.

"Let's find out," said Job. He cupped his dark hands to his mouth and hollered "Hello, the house!"

His call seemed to fall on deaf ears at first. Then the door opened and someone stepped out on the porch.

It was an elderly woman, perhaps eighty years or older. She was as stooped and thin as a willow tree and the skin of her face and hands was heavily wrinkled and burnished a tanned brown by sun and age. Her hair was thin and as white as the snow that graced the ground, and she was dressed in a faded gingham dress with a knitted shawl across her narrow shoulders. The woman's eyes, though, were as blue as sapphires and belied a savvy and intelligence that went far beyond even her advanced years.

She would have seemed completely harmless and helpless, except for a double-barreled ten-gauge shotgun with flintlock hammers on each side of the breech. "I hear ya," she said evenly. She lifted the gun until it was directed at the two riders. The muzzles of the scattergun looked as big as cannon bores. "You friend or foe? If you're the latter and up to no good, I'll just go ahead and blow you outta those saddles right now and store you in the smokehouse yonder till the ground's thawed enough for burying."

"We come with the most honorable of intentions, ma'am," Job assured her. "I reckon it's Granny Marigold who I'm speaking to?"

The old woman nodded and sent a spritz of tobacco juice to the porch floor. "That I be."

"Marigold like the flower?" Dead-Eye asked.

She frowned sourly. "That's right. My ma bore five daughters and she named every one after the blossoms in her garden. Rose, Lily, Iris, Violet. Of the bunch, she had the audacity to name me after a stinky flower that smelled like a cross between a polecat and unwashed ass."

Job studied her sagely. "I'd say you're a granny woman, ain't you?"

"And you'd be right," she agreed. The shotgun remained on them, unwavering from its aim. "I'm a practitioner of mountain spells, salves, and potions. Learnt my trade from my mama and grandmama at an early age. I've got something for about anything that ails or vexes you. Is that why you're here? You're in need of my services?"

"No, ma'am," said the tall Southerner. "Just passing through."

"How'd you hear tell of me then?"

"A feller over on Blood Moon Ridge told us."

Granny Marigold shook her aged head in disgust. "Damned town full of fools and heathens is what it is. So, are you gonna sit there and gawk, or are you gonna put those critters in the barn and come in for a bite to eat?"

"We're obliged for the invitation, dear lady," Job told her with a tip of his derby hat.

The old woman arched an eyebrow and grinned thinly. "Most men with that fine a set of manners usually have some hidden motive for being that way. You figuring to take advantage of Ol' Granny and jump the mattress with her?"

"Certainly not!" said the black man, disturbed by the notion. "I have the utmost respect and discretion toward you, Miss Marigold."

Granny spat juice again and scowled. "Aw, shit!" She seemed disappointed by his honorable intentions. "Well, might as well come in and sit a spell anyways."

The two rode their mounts to the barn across the road and left them in two stalls inside. Then they trudged back to the cabin and let themselves in. Granny was at an iron pot suspended over the flames of the hearth. She dipped a wooden spoon into the contents and tasted it. "Hope y'all take to soup, 'cause that's all there is. Sit at the table yonder and I'll dip it up."

They took a seat and looked around the interior of the cabin. The only furnishings were the table and chairs, a rickety rocking chair, and a big brass bed in a far corner loaded with heavy patchwork quilts. From the rafters hung all manner of animal hides, medicinal roots, and dried plants.

Before the elderly woman could dip up a third bowl, Dead-Eye spoke up. "No need to serve me, Granny. I don't partake of nourishment."

"How come?" she asked, unconcerned. "'Cause you're dead?"

"Most folks overlook that fact, or are too damn stupid to figure it out," the gunfighter said.

"I've heard tell of your kind, but never seen one with my own eyes. A *zombie*, ain't that the proper term?"

"That it is," Job told her pridefully.

"And you're the one who conjured him, is that right?" she asked. Granny studied the charms that hung about his neck. "I reckon you're a swamp shaman or such?"

"A mojo man from the dark heart of Louisiana. Also a purveyor of the mystical arts, same as you are."

"And you're looking for a soulless blood-sucker named Jules Holland and his followers," she stated as she sat a steaming bowl of soup and a china cup of coffee before him.

Job was startled. "Now how in tarnation did you know that?"

"I had me a dream nearly a week ago," she explained. "A nightmare full of horror and misery over things they had done and will do. Then a few days ago, they rode through on their way to Keyhole Pass and the valley below. It was past dusk and the vampire was astride a horse along with that hellish trio of his. And your daughter was driving a pitch-black wagon drawn by a team of two."

"My daughter?"

"She wore a veil, but I could see the shape of her face, the set of her eyes, and the bones of her cheeks. They were the same as yours, mojo man." Then the old woman turned her eyes to Dead-Eye. "And there was a young'un with her. A boy... tall and lean... the spitting image of you at a younger age."

"Daniel," the gunfighter whispered beneath his breath.

"Yes. And the child grieved, for both his ma and pa were dead. And that's the truth of it, isn't it?"

"Indeed," admitted Dead-Eye. "On both counts."

The old woman turned her eyes to Job. "Funny thing... the witch... that girl of your'n... she gave me the evil eye the whole time they rode by. I think she knew what I was; that I held skills and knowings the same as she. Then, when they were nearly out of sight, it turned from the balm of an Indian summer to a cold and blustery winter's night. It commenced to snowing and it's done so on and off ever since. I believe it was of her doing, too. We've never had this much snowfall before the end of the year, as far back as I can recall."

Job looked over at Dead-Eye and nodded. They both remembered the stormy night back in Skullbone, Tennessee, when rain and lightning drove them into a barn full of vampires.

The three grew silent. Job ate his soup, aware that Granny Marigold appraised him with interest and, perhaps, even lust.

"You know, I've been married six times in my eighty-seven years," she told him. "But I've never had me no African man before."

"And you shan't now, either," said the mojo man, searching for something to change the subject. "You know, this here soup would be better with a little beef or chicken."

"Ain't got neither," she told him. "All my hens died of an ailment and I'm too old to get out and hunt. I saw a big ol' buck or two in the meadow yonder. This tall gunman here could fetch me deer for venison, while you stay here and keep me company."

Job laughed humorlessly. "I'm aware of what kinda company you're referring to. And it's still not gonna happen."

"If the iron's gone outta your nail, I've got a potion for you to drink…"

"Don't need any confounded potion to boost my masculinity, thank you!" the mojo man declared.

She looked over at the other man. "How's about you? I'd bet you're a stiff one."

Dead-Eye looked at her. "Ma'am, I'm pretty much stiff all over these days."

Job lifted his bowl and drank the dregs of his soup. "You'll get your venison for the winter, but I'll be going with him on the hunt."

Granny shrugged. "Suit yourself. But you could be pleasuring in a warm bed rather than freezing your ass in a saddle. It's your choice." She nodded toward the fireplace. "Take that old Hawken rifle over the mantlepiece there. It shoots straight and true. It would bring a bear down if the right shooter was behind it."

Dead-Eye walked over and took the .50-caliber rifle from its cradle, along with a horn of powder and a possible bag stocked with lead balls, patches, and grease for lubing. "I reckon I can handle it well enough."

Soon, Job slipped his coat on and was accompanying Dead-Eye outside, leaving Granny Marigold inside. The mojo man looked downright anxious to be away from the cabin.

"Horny ol' gal, ain't she?" said the gunfighter with a wry grin upon his gaunt face.

"Stuck out here in the boonies and awful lonesome for a man, that's what she is. Of course, upon seeing me, who can blame her. I tend to have such an amorous effect on members of the female persuasion, both young and old. It's truly a curse, it is."

"Yeah, I'm sure they get all hot and bothered, particularly when they see a scrawny, little feller with a head as slick as a billiard ball and a mouth full of gold and silver teeth that would shame a bank into foreclosure."

"Let's fetch Brimstone and Balaam and commence to getting that venison," said Job, looking to change the subject. The flurry of snowflakes that swirled in the gray sky quickened and grew heavier. "I was aiming to ask her if we could spend the night, but I'm thinking better of it now. Better do what we're setting out to do and then head for the Keyhole before the snowfall strands us."

"Are you sure you don't want to stick around and bump uglies with Miss Marigold yonder? You've been awful melancholy and down in the mouth lately. Could uplift your outlook considerably."

"I'd just as soon mount a hollow log full of bees," Job declared. "Now let's get out there and find that buck, before I think better of it and lift that spell that keeps you walking and talking. You keep poking fun and I'll be tempted to do just that!"

Dead-Eye said nothing else on the delicate subject and, soon, the two were in the saddle, heading across the snowy expanse of Blue Sky Meadow, in search of Granny's winter venison.

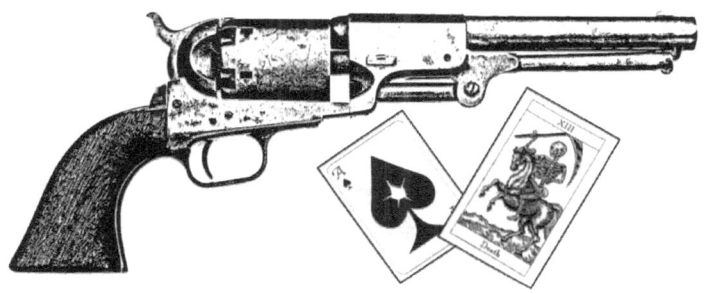

Chapter Seven

Granny Marigold's Cabin
Mid-November 1866

By the time they returned, it was night and a blizzard was upon them. Their search for wild game had seemed to be a hopeless endeavor at first. The snowy pastures that ran along the spine of the mountaintop appeared devoid of life, as though the unexpected onset of an early winter had driven the wildlife to the concealment of shelter or onward to a warmer climate. Eventually, they spotted a few jackrabbits and a red fox on the prowl. Dead-Eye refrained from dispatching them, for the big .50-caliber would have rendered them useless, with little meat left to salvage.

Dusk was deepening when they finally happened on a large whitetail buck. It was a majestic animal with a rack totaling fourteen points in all. The Southerner sighted steadily down the octagon barrel of the Hawken and dropped him with a single shot through the heart.

They bound the animal to Balaam and Job stuck the rifle in one of the canvas packs for safekeeping, then slung the leather bag and powder horn over his shoulder. Together, the two men headed back to Granny's place. Halfway there, the gentle snow that had fallen throughout most of the day picked up with gale and fury, changing from a flurry to a stinging, blinding blizzard. The snow upon the ground increased from six inches to nearly a foot in a short period of time, hindering their progress. Also, it was difficult to navigate in the thickening snowfall. The air around them turned into a wall of swirling ice, blinding them to what lay only a few yards ahead.

"Do you believe Evangeline had a hand in conjuring this, like Granny said?" Dead-Eye asked. As the evening darkened into night, his blind eye—illuminated by the foxfire that the outlaw named Boar had ground cruelly into the orb—cast a pale, yellow glow ahead of them. However, the wind and snow were so furious and unceasing, that it did very little to assist them in their passage.

"I wouldn't doubt it," said Job. He hunkered down in Balaam's saddle, sheltered by the coat of many hides and his bowler hat. "She has access to magic and conjuring that I don't. Particularly if she recruited some being from the Hole Out of Nowhere who has command over wind and weather."

As they traveled due north, the night deepened around them. Through the relentless snowfall, a glow cut through the fury and they looked up to see a hint of circular light high above them.

"The full moon," indicated Dead-Eye. He swept his coat to the side, revealing the butt of the Dragoon angled across his belly. Bones crackled and tendons creaked like worn leather as he flexed his frozen hand, shedding the ice that had collected there.

"Yes," said Job. He pulled the silver dagger from his sleeve and looked about him. A dark shape, barely discernible in the curtain of snow, flashed across their path and then was gone. "I'm beginning to think we should have ended our hunt and gotten back to Granny's before nightfall."

"I reckon so." Dead-Eye felt Brimstone tense beneath him. The Morgan's eyes glowed red like muted coals and his body grew increasingly warm, as though a fire was kindled beneath his hide. The gunfighter shucked the Colt from its holster and swung the sawed-off shotgun from the concealment of his coat.

The white mule grew skittish. He snorted and blew frosty breath through his nostrils. Two more forms leapt through the icy gloom, then vanished just as quickly. "We're surrounded," said the mojo man, just loud enough for his traveling partner to hear.

Dead-Eye peered through the darting snow ahead and saw a pale, yellow glow in the distance. The window of a house. "There's the cabin!" he called out. "Let's make a run for it!" He spurred his mount with the heels of his boots. The black horse surged forward at a gallop.

Job took heed and, soon, Balaam matched the Morgan in its stride.

The dark structure of the barn loomed out of the blizzard and they knew they only had a hundred yards or so to go. Abruptly, a dark, hirsute form leapt from the roof of the barn with a coarse growl. The creature hit Dead-Eye hard, driving him from the saddle. The zombie landed on his back in the snow, but kept hold of his weapons. The werewolf landed on its feet and stood over the dead man. Its savage face leered in the glow of Dead-Eye's blind eye—fangs bared, eyes red and full of bloodlust. And there was something else there as well. A hunger for vengeance for some grave wrong done to kith or kin.

Dead-Eye snapped off a shot with a boom of his pistol. The monster jerked its head to the side before the silver slug could burrow into its snout. Before the projectile was lost in the darkness, it grazed the edge of the wolf's ear. The furrow smoked and sputtered as the flesh singed upon contact. The creature threw back its massive head and howled, then reached down and grabbed the gunfighter by the shirtfront, hauling him to his feet. Long claws punctured the white silk and raked against dead flesh.

Not my damn shirt again! he thought as the wolf reared back with his right arm, intending to decapitate him with a single swipe.

However, before it could do so, Brimstone's glowing eyes appeared behind him. Heat and cinder exploded from the demon horse's open mouth, catching the brute's fur on fire. Aflame, it released Dead-Eye and stumbled away. As it dropped to the ground with a cry and rolled in the snow, attempting to extinguish itself, the Southerner thumbed back the right hammer of the scattergun and put a silver slug through the small of its back.

Hellfire! thought Dead-Eye, quite literally.

Job and Balaam were fifty feet or so ahead of it. "Make a run for the cabin!" the negro shouted over the howl of the wind.

The gunslinger intended to swing atop Brimstone, but the horse was already plunging into the swirling snowfall after another beast. With a curse, Dead-Eye took to running. The snow was twelve inches or so deep in the barnyard, so it was slow going.

Up ahead, a slender beast with light blond fur leapt in front of Balaam. The mule came to a skidding halt, throwing his master out of the saddle in the process. Job would have probably broken a bone, if a snowdrift hadn't cushioned the impact.

The light-furred werewolf snarled and went for the equally-pale mule. Dead-Eye saw pendulous breasts, signifying that the beast was female in gender. He instantly thought of the waitress at the restaurant... the one with the corn silk hair.

He lifted his Dragoon to take aim, but never got the chance to fire. Before he could, Balaam reared on his back hooves and brought the front ones down forcefully. One collided with the top of the werewolf's skull. Its silver shoe sank into flesh and bone like a hot knife through freshly-churned butter. Brain matter, blackened and smoldering, exploded from the wound as the beast released a death cry and sank to its knees. The mule's momentum fairly cleaved its attacker's head in half, before he pulled away and pawed the gore from his hoof in the snow.

A moment later, Dead-Eye had Job on his feet and both were headed in the direction of the cabin. The square of light grew closer and clearer with every step they took. Several times, wolfish forms loomed out of the thick snowfall, only to be driven back by a well-placed shot from the .44 Dragoon or a swipe from the mojo man's silver-bladed knife.

"What about Brimstone and Balaam?" he asked, glancing over his shoulder. The forms of the horse and mule could barely be seen through the icy veil, fending off attacks from their hirsute assailants. The gunfighter got off one last shot before the hammer snapped on an empty chamber. Then he holstered the pistol and concentrated on making the porch of the mountain cabin before they were taken down.

"Leave 'em be," Job told him. He lurched and limped on his left foot. Apparently, he had sprained or broken his ankle during his spill from the saddle. "Looks like they can hold their own. We'd best be worrying about our own hides for now!"

They were a dozen feet from the log cabin when a tall, gangly wolf rushed in, swinging his long, lean-muscled arms like a farmer's scythe. Before they could react, the creature attacked Dead-Eye. The dead man caught a glimpse of a long, wolfish face… its dark whiskers streaked with gray. The beast slashed out savagely and, with claws as long as camp knives, sliced the gunfighter's right arm away at the shoulder. The limb fell into the snow, twitching and squirming.

Job jabbed with his dagger, stabbing the werewolf—which had a peculiar resemblance to Gabel Bruley—midway between breastbone and navel. The creature howled in agony as it turned and loped away.

A moment later, they wrenched open the cabin door and were inside. Job slammed it shut and barred it with a long length of hickory wood that sat nearby for such a purpose.

They turned to see Granny Marigold sitting in her rocking chair before the hearth, covered from chin to knees in a wedding ring quilt. Her face seemed completely unconcerned as she regarded the two. "Took you two long enough to get back."

"Granny, there's some ungodly critters out there!" Dead-Eye told her.

The elderly woman nodded. "Yessir, I know that. Werewolves." She examined the pair from head to toe. "Looks like you got past 'em, though." Her ancient eyes settled on the ragged stump of the gunfighter's shoulder. "Well, *most* of you, anyhow."

"I'm betting it was those Bruleys," Job said, catching his breath.

"Yeah. Them and everyone else on Blood Moon Ridge. They've all been cursed with the bite of the Beast."

"Well, I'll be damned!" exclaimed the mojo man. Something suddenly dawned on him. "That yeller-haired wolf…"

"Was that gal that served you in the restaurant," Dead-Eye told him. "Figured that out for myself."

"I'd say y'all better get over to that window yonder and load your guns," the granny woman suggested. "They're not going away until they have their fill of you."

The two did as she said. Dead-Eye crouched next to the cabin's front window, while Job unlatched the shutters and opened them wide. There were no glass panes in the window, so they had full access to those who invaded Blue Sky Meadow. But, unfortunately, it also gave the hillbilly lycanthropes full access to them as well.

"The mangy bastard ripped my arm off!" grumbled Dead-Eye. "How am I supposed to shoot without my right hand?"

"Believe me, you can shoot just as well with your left. Just give it a try."

Awkwardly, the gunfighter drew the big Dragoon and grimaced. "I'm sure missing that arm. Look at it yonder, lying in the snow. It's gonna get all frozen up!"

"What's dead can't be frostbitten," Job assured him. "Now quit your pouting and get ready! They'll be upon the house before we know it."

Dead-Eye couldn't seem to rid it from his mind, though. "What if one of those critters devours it?"

"Well, if it does, we'll just fetch you another one. Stop off at a funeral parlor or graveyard on the way out of town and pick out a real nice one. How does that sound?"

"I'd rather have the one I was born with. Doesn't seem proper walking around with another man's arm, or, heaven forbid, a *woman's*!"

"I do declare, you're the most exasperating son of a bitch I've ever come across!" said Job. "If I'd known you were so contrary, I would've buried you in that clearing back in Tennessee and been on my way."

"Just hush and load my pistol for me, will you?" Dead-Eye told him with a glare. "Can't do it one-handed."

Job did as he asked, digging twelve paper cartridges of powder and silver ball from the Southerner's coat pocket. He bit off the ends with his precious metal teeth and soon had each of the Dragoon's six chambers loaded, packed, and the firing nipples capped. "Where the hell's your shotgun?" he demanded.

"Out yonder next to my arm. It slipped off my shoulder, 'cause there was nothing there for the sling to perch on."

"That's just dandy!" said the mojo man. "Got more revolver ammunition in your other pocket?"

"No, just shotgun shells. Don't you have any with you? You made two or three dozen."

It was Job's turn to be embarrassed. "Hell no! They're stashed in Balaam's pack out there somewhere."

"I reckon we'll just have to make do with what we've got." Dead-Eye looked toward Granny sitting next to the fireplace. "Exactly how many folks live over in Blood Moon?"

"Oh, not many," she told him. "Maybe forty or fifty at the most."

The zombie and the mojo man looked at one another. They didn't have nearly enough silver bullets to take them all down. In fact, maybe a quarter of the beasts at the most. After that, the silver dagger was their only weapon of defense.

Dead-Eye laid the elbow of his left arm across the bottom sill of the open window, steadying his aim and watching for darting shapes in the blizzard. "I reckon I'd best commence to shooting," he said. A disgruntled frown showed beneath his thick, black mustache. "But I'd rather be shooting with my other arm. Feels peculiar resorting to this one."

"Forget your confounded arm and just shoot the damn gun!"

Dead-Eye peered through the open window, sighting the big hogleg and squeezing off a shot every time a dark form could be seen amid the earthbound snowfall. More than often there was a grunt as the projectiles hit and a howl of agony and despair as the silver poisoned their cursed bloodstream. A few times, though, they dodged the shots and the silver arched off into the icy night, useless and wasted.

When the last shot was fired, Dead-Eye turned to the negro. "Gun's empty. What do we do now?"

Job shrugged. "I've got this here horn of powder and you've got a tin of percussion caps in your pocket, but we've got no silver left to fight with."

Suddenly, a massive, brown-furred wolf leapt upon the porch and swiped through the open window. Its claws knocked off Dead-Eye's hat and nearly scalped him. Job flicked his wrist and the silver knife spun, handle over blade. The dagger impaled the beast's left eye, piercing the orb and sinking deeply into the brain beyond. The creature wailed and stumbled backward, its immortality compromised by the mojo man's throwing skill. Sluggishly, it yanked the knife from its eye socket and flung it to the boards of the porch, then disappeared into the blizzard. The weapon lay there, in sight, but out of reach.

"Granny!" called Job desperately. "You got any silver hereabouts? Maybe beads or such?" He knew that there was a chance that she might have something of the sort for making charms and talismans.

"Sorry," the old woman told him. She began to shiver beneath the patchwork quilt, as though in the throes of a fever chill. "Got nary a speck of it in the house a'tall."

Dead-Eye thought about it for a moment, then turned to his companion. "Smile."

Job frowned. "What?"

"I said *smile!*"

The little man shook his head in puzzlement, then split a big grin.

Without hesitation, the gunslinger clouted Job across the mouth forcefully with the heavy barrel of the Dragoon, knocking most of the teeth from his mouth. Gold and silver dropped and rattled across the dusty floorboards.

"What the shit did you do that for?" hollered Job in alarm.

Dead-Eye handed him the pistol with his only hand. "Pick through those teeth and find the silver ones. Then load 'er up!"

Despite the pain, Job did what he asked, knowing it could be their only chance. Soon, he had all six chambers loaded with powder and silver teeth. The tall Southerner took the gun and began firing again.

When all the silver was used up, the two looked at one another. "I'd say there's at least fifteen or twenty left out there," said Dead-Eye. "Looks like we're done for."

Abruptly, sounds drew their attention and they turned to regard Granny Marigold. The elderly woman was shivering and shaking beneath her quilt. Her head pitched back and forth and her ancient eyes had rolled back in her head until only the whites remained.

"She's having a fit of some sort!" said Job fearfully. Granny's amorous attentions had annoyed him, but he still thought well of the old woman and hated to see her succumb to a failed heart or a brain stroke.

"No," Dead-Eye told him. "Much worse than that."

The two watched as Granny Marigold's head began to broaden from ear to ear, and lengthen from the back of her skull to the tip of her nose. Her ears sharpened into points, growing long and erect, and her nose and upper lip joined with a crackle of cartilage and bone, slowly changing into the elongated snout of a timber wolf. Her jaw unhinged and a long scream of agony changed pitch in mid-shout, turning into a throaty howl. Within her mouth, naked gums sprouted jagged points of bone. They quickly lengthened into fangs as long as a man's middle finger.

Tossing the bedcovers away, the old woman stood from her chair. Her stooped body contorted and flexed. The bones of her humerus and femur grew long, adding height and reach to her diminutive form. Her hands cracked and popped, the bones breaking and then reforming. Her short fingernails grew, inch by inch, until wicked claws evolved, sharp enough to carve meat from the bone.

"Good God Almighty!" moaned Job. "She's one of them!"

Dead-Eye nodded grimly. "And now she's coming for *us!*"

They retreated until their backs were to the wall as Granny tore across the cabin floor, heading straight for them. However, right when they were certain that she would rip them into shreds, the white-haired werewolf passed them and leapt through the open window into the churning blizzard.

Job closed the shutters and secured them. Beyond the wooden

panels they could hear snapping and snarling as Granny and the other lycanthropes clashed and fought. Howls of suffering and defeat rang through the night, cutting through the wailing of the wind. They knew none of the death cries belonged to the old mountain witch, for her deep-throated snarls and howls continued as she encountered one brute after another.

The mojo man left his place on the floor and walked toward the hearth.

"Where are you going?" asked Dead-Eye.

"To stoke the fire," Job told him. "I'd say we have a long, bloody night ahead of us."

Daybreak brought an end to the blizzard and yellow sunlight blazed over the peaks of the Ozarks, striking the heavy drifts so brightly that it would nearly blind a man to look at it. Here and there in the snowfall were mounds where bodies lay buried beneath the surface; no longer the beasts they had been the night before, but men and women who were now blessed with the unburdening of their curse and the silent, still comfort of death.

Granny Marigold appeared from a grove of pines and stumbled toward the cabin. She was naked, her pendulous breasts sagging to her bellybutton and swaying from side to side as she walked. Mercifully, Job met her halfway across the yard with the patchwork quilt and covered her scrawny, blue-fleshed body.

When they got back inside the house, the old woman shuddered violently. Even before the roaring hearth, she could find no warmth. "I'm chilled to the very marrow of my bones!" she said hoarsely, launching into a fit of coughing. Her aged eyes cut to Job slyly. "I can think of one thing that might thaw me out, though."

Job swallowed bitterly. *Lord Jesus! Here she goes again!*

"Why don't you send Ol' Dead-Puss there out to the barn to tend to the critters? Then me and you'n can slip 'neath the covers yonder and start us a fire, like two skinny sticks rubbing together."

"I'm much obliged for the offer, Granny," Job told her, "but the last time I jacked the springs with a white woman, it bought me a world of trouble, along with a brood of no-account young'uns… one of them being a galldurned witch with an appetite for destruction. I'm not about to make that mistake a second time."

Granny scowled and nodded in defeat. She plopped into her rocking chair with a creaking of weathered wood and old bones, and gathered the quilt tighter about her.

Dead-Eye regarded her with curiosity. "If you were one of those were-critters, why did you jump out there and fight the others? Why didn't you just pounce upon and eat us?"

"A couple of reasons, really," she told him. "First off, I don't regard nasty, dead things as nourishing vittles." She looked over at Job. "Secondly, I never did develop a taste for dark meat."

Job shucked his hat off his bald head and held it reverently against his breast. "For that simple blessing, I'll bypass the Great Creator and pray thanks to the gods of my distant ancestry for the divine privilege of my nightshade complexion."

"Another reason is that you both are decent folk who I've taken a liking to," Granny continued. "And, to tell the honest truth, it was high time I up and did something about that ornery bunch of Bruleys. They've been a nest of chiggers up my hind end for many a year!"

"I think I'll fix up a pan of biscuits and a skillet of hog jowl and we'll have us a bite of breakfast," Job said. "Maybe getting some flour and grease in your belly will kindle your temperature. Then Dead-Eye and I will ready our hosses and head on out."

"I'm too full of nasty-ass hillbillies," Granny told him. "One more bite and I'd bust. And I'm afeared that you're plumb stuck where you be. Keyhole is the only pass down out of these mountains and it's likely eight foot deep with snow. My bones tell me there's another storm rolling through in an hour or two, with a good foot or more to add to it. You likely won't be going nowhere till spring thaw in March."

"Well, ain't that a shitty hand to be dealt," said Dead-Eye.

Job couldn't help but feel badly about it as well. "Why, Holland and his gang will be four hundred miles away by then. And how am I supposed to eat with scarcely a tooth left in my skull? Not that it matters. We'll likely all starve to death before it's over and done with."

"Now, don't worry your shiny head over that none," Granny assured him. "There's that venison you brought back from the meadow, and canned vittles in the root cellar beneath the house, as well as hay and feed aplenty out yonder in the barn. Ain't nobody gonna lose a meal while visiting Granny Marigold!"

"Well, I don't eat, so I don't give a damn either way," said Dead-Eye. He opened the door to step outside. "I'm gonna take a walk and hunt down that arm of mine "

Job nodded. "You do that. Dig that limb out of the ice and we'll thaw it out and mend it back in place. I'm sure Granny has a sewing box hereabouts somewhere."

"I surely do." She regarded the mojo man. "And if the loss of your teeth bothers you so, I can do the job myself. For half my life, I've been the only dentist for a hundred miles in these parts. Y'all gather up the gold ones and dig the silver ones out of those carcasses yonder and I'll put them back in. Got some salve made of snakeroot, goldenseal, and pokeweed that'll open up the root holes in those gums of yours. They'll latch onto those teeth, good as new, like a babe tight on its mammy's teat." She grinned lecherously with shiny pink gums. "For a fee that is." She eyed Job, then turned her gaze to the big brass bed in the corner.

The mojo man sighed. "You're just not gonna take leave of that hankering, are you?"

"No, sir! The feeling's upon me and likely won't be quelling till the first bloom of spring. And for the dentistry chore, it'll be payment in advance."

"Lord, woman, you do strike a hard bargain." Job shook his head in resignation and, shedding his many-pocketed vest, slipped the suspenders off his narrow shoulders. "If it be so, let's get it done. I ain't much at all without my winning smile and sunny disposition, and I'm willing to sacrifice my integrity to earn them back. Besides, couldn't be no harm in indulging, since you're far past your prime and beyond fertility."

Granny laughed loudly, leaving her chair. "You speak for yourself."

Dead-Eye shook his head. "Well, I'll not lay witness to such doings," he declared. "I'm already blind in one eye. Ain't about to damn the other."

And, with that, he ducked outside, in search of his lost appendage.

Chapter Eight

The Indian Territory
April 1867

It had been a long hard winter.

Following the werewolf attack on Blue Sky Meadow, the snowfall continued as November lapsed into December, scarcely ending for an hour or two at a time. Dense snowdrifts piled along the walls and windows of Granny Marigold's cabin, as well as the outbuildings around it. One morning, they awoke to find that the snow had accumulated so tightly against the front door, that opening it was impossible. They had taken a hatchet and broken open a section of the roof for the purpose of tending to the animals in the barn and fetching water from the creek a quarter mile away.

Days were spent in idle talk, performing menial chores, or indulging in games of chance at the eating table. Job was an exceptional hand with poker, but Granny could bet, blind, and bluff with the best of them. In time, the two developed a genuine friendship that extended beyond card-playing or an occasional tryst beneath the quilts. Combining their knowledge of conjuring and rural magic, the two worked to concoct some way to stop the onset of the uncharacteristic weather. But, if Evangeline had somehow cast an icy spell upon the Ozarks to thwart Dead-Eye and Job's pursuit, they had no idea how to reverse or bring it to a halt.

Dead-Eye would sometimes sit in the crackling glow of the hearth while the others slept. Often, he would hear Job speak to Marigold softly in the dark, offering to end the curse that imprisoned her in the body of a beast with each rise of the full moon.

"I was bitten when I was seventeen years of age," she would tell him. "It has been a part of my body and soul for nearly seventy years. Even though my youth and beauty have faded with age, I feel no pain or sorrow, no lament or loss, when I am in that form. I am free, with no regret of being so."

The thaw began with the second week of spring and, soon, the hard-packed snow began to melt away and the land underneath was laid bare. Dead-Eye and Job saddled their mounts and said their goodbyes to Granny Marigold. The old woman granted a parting gift to Job—a satchel of medicinal herbs and powders for healing, and a forked hickory branch for divining water. Before long, they headed down the trail and found the narrow canyon of Keyhole Pass unobstructed by ice and snow. Carefully, they made their way along a steep, winding trail to the bottomland below.

As March surrendered to April, they made their way across the state of Arkansas. They discovered evidence of Holland and his gang's passage as they moved from town to town. In Fayetteville, they heard tales of folks who had crossed paths with the outlaws and disappeared. Later, those folks were seen wandering through the town cemetery at night. They seemed to be trapped in a frightening state between life and death, neither alive nor dead.

In Fort Smith, a church picnic had been engulfed in black fire and the entire congregation had perished in the unholy blaze. The townsfolk regarded the churchyard as cursed and refused to set foot upon it. As they rode past, Dead-Eye and Job could see the charred bodies of families sitting beneath the burnt and leafless trees. The peculiar ebony fire still crackled and guttered in places, as if originating from recesses beneath the earth. No one had gathered the nerve to bury the poor souls in fear of ending up the same way.

In a saloon, they discovered that Holland's men had been overheard at a corner table, discussing their intentions of traveling to New Orleans. The riders and the woman driving the black wagon had crossed over into the Indian Territory, then headed south. The gunslinger and the mojo man bought supplies for the journey, then crossed the border as well, anxious to be on their way.

They had ridden several days across flat, desolate terrain, when something ahead stopped them in their tracks. It was a small circle of black the size of a silver dollar hanging, suspended, in the air, six feet from the ground. The edges of the hole crackled with blue sparks as it spun slowly, then gathered speed.

"You reckon that's…?" Job began.

Dead-Eye nodded grimly. "The Hole Out of Nowhere. Wonder who's coming to call this time?"

They sat on their mounts and waited as the hole gradually widened and lengthened until the bottom of the portal met the earth. From the darkness within emanated a warm dankness and a nasty stench like the killing floor of a slaughterhouse. Then, from within, someone emerged.

The being was tall, perhaps seven feet in height or more. He was dressed in a long, black cloak that extended from his narrow shoulders to his ankles, and upon his head was an equally black hat, flat brimmed and rounded at the peak like a Quaker's. There was no flesh or muscle upon his face or frame. Only bones, slickened with blood and gore, shown from within his dark clothing. Beneath the shadow of his hat, the fiend's skull leered, grinning. The sockets of its eyes were black and bottomless, like the pit of some infinite well. Around his lean waist was a sash and bag, and he held a long scythe in one skeletal hand, also constructed of bone and dipped in glistening ichor.

"Who the hell are you?" asked Dead-Eye flatly.

"I am Alkor Rank, the Bone Harvester," he said. His voice was coarse and had a peculiar, melodic ring to it, like wind whistling through the hollow of empty, marrowless bone.

"That's a mouthful to be referred to," the zombie told him. "Being dead and all, my memory for names is a mite faulty. I reckon I'll just call you Bloody Bones instead."

The gunfighter's statement seemed to vex him. "I am not a tale told to frighten young children into submission or favorable behavior! You have no notion of the thousands I have conquered, both in my realm and your own. Mongolian raiders, Roman Centurions, Greek Argonauts… all have fallen beneath the sweep of my blade and the armies I have sown and brought forth."

"And you were sent to confront and defeat us?" asked Job. "By who?"

"The enchantress Evangeline warranted your demise," Alkor Rank told him.

"And for what payment? Our souls?"

The crimson skeleton laughed. "I have no want for souls. My needs are more substantial… more physical than existential. Upon your deaths, I shall split your flesh and claim your bones for my bounty. To build the structures and pave the streets of my kingdom, as I have done generation upon generation before."

"Sorry," said Dead-Eye, "but we wouldn't get much further without a frame with which to hold us up." He drew the Colt Dragoon from its holster and held it aloft, barrel pointed skyward. "Now crawl back into that stink hole of yours and allow us to be on our way."

Alkor Rank found humor in the threat. His mirth boomed across the open prairie like the rumble of thunder. "I believe not, fool. The end of your passage is nigh. I shall depart only with your bone and life, and you shall lay flaccid and defeated upon the ground where you stand."

"I reckon I could empty this here pistol into you and reduce you to a broken heap with no trouble a'tall," Dead-Eye told him. "Now, do as I say. Back off!"

The Bone Harvester shook his bloody skull, weary of their resistance. "Your petty weapon with its fire and smoke and impotent load will do me no harm. I shall call forth the dead of the earth and they shall fight for me. Those who have tasted the bitter wine of death and can die no more."

Alkor Rank's slender arms emerged from the sleeves of his black cloak and, wielding the scythe, he dug a long furrow in the dry, hard dirt of the land. He then took the black bag from his sash and opened it. His bloody hand dipped inside, bringing forth a generous fistful of what looked to be human teeth. Carefully, he sowed the bits of bone into the depths of the furrow and covered the dirt over with the flat of his blade.

"This is sacred ground upon which we stand," the Harvester told them. "Trodden by a displaced people of noble blood. Men, women, and children driven from their homes by the hatred of the pale-fleshed man. They marched under duress, mile upon mile, and many fell to despair and disease, upon their mournful trail of tears. Those who I call forth were mighty warriors... the protectors and slayers of their tribe. As they shall slay you now and end the trail upon which you travel."

"Can't say that I like what this is amounting to," said the mojo man beneath his breath. He watched the earth where the teeth had been planted. It was still at first. Then the dirt began to slowly buckle and rise.

Dead-Eye and Job watched as the ground broke open and skeletal forms burst forth, unfolding, then standing tall and erect in the warm sun of the April day. Their fleshless skulls were painted brightly with the hues of war and, from the stone and shale of the earth, were formed weapons— spears, knives, tomahawks, and tautly-strung bows. Soon, a dozen stood and confronted them, crouching, at the ready. Eager to attack and conquer.

Slowly, the twelve advanced, their bony fists clutching weapons of destruction, ready to deal death and defeat. They took several steps, then three of the bunch attacked. Two threw spear and hatchet with unerring precision, while a third unlimbered his bow and, producing arrows from its own bone, fired one projectile after another.

Before the weapons reached their intended targets, Brimstone turned, shielding Job and Balaam from harm. Arrows pierced the Morgan's black hide, anchoring deeply into his neck, belly, and haunches. The demon horse paid them no mind and stood his ground. Dead-Eye fanned the hammer of the forty-four, emptying the pistol's chambers, before a flint-headed spear pierced his right shoulder, causing him to lose hold of the gun. The blade of the tomahawk sank into the putrid meat of his right thigh and remained anchored there.

His bullets found the places they were intended for, shattering the joints of elbows and knees of the warriors. Four collapsed into a heap, but it wasn't long before the bones had rejuvenated and they once again stood tall, ready to fight. A painted skeleton rushed in, sporting a long-bladed knife in each fist. Dead-Eye swung his twelve-gauge from beneath his coat and fired both barrels. The shot hit the warrior in the chest, shattering his breastbone and caving in his ribs. The skeleton staggered backward a few steps, then snapped its toothy jaws in defiance. Dead-Eye watched as the bones of the ribcage and sternum knitted together quickly and were whole again.

"Well, shooting 'em ain't gonna do a speck of good," said Job from behind him. An instant later, his quick wit advised him of what course should be taken. "Tell me… which way does the wind blow?"

The gunfighter licked his forefinger and held it to the air. "To the south… towards them."

"Then clear my path."

As Dead-Eye and Brimstone moved to the side, Job spurred the mule forward and faced the advancing tribe. He reached up and yanked a small, green-glass bottle from the necklace of hoodoo charms around his neck. He crushed the bottle between his fingers, filling his palm with a fine green powder.

"The Book of Ezekiel saith!" The mojo man's voice rang out, bold and steady. "And the hand of the Lord was upon me, and set me down in the midst of the valley which was full of bones… and caused me to pass by them round about, and behold, there were very many and, lo, they were very dry…"

Job raised his hand above his head and the green dust left his palm and took wing on the breeze. As it drifted southward, the powder grew bright and thick, expanding into a cloud the closer it came to the advancing war party.

"And He said unto me, prophesy upon these bones, and say unto them, O ye dry bones, hear the word of the Lord!"

Soon, the green powder reached the attacking skeletons. It clung to their exposed bones, coating their skulls and all that lay beneath. The substance gradually began to thicken, growing from green to raw, blood red, similar to the color of their cloaked master. They slowed their stalking and faltered, clearly confused at what was taking place.

"And I will lay sinews upon you, and bring up flesh upon you, and cover you with skin, and put breath in you, and ye shall live!"

The being known as Alkor Rank took a guarded step backward as he witnessed the bizarre transformation that was taking place. The reddening substance upon the skeletons traveled the length of their lanky frames, flourishing with new muscle and sinew. The dark pits of their skulls filled with membrane and tissue and eyes abruptly stared from the hollows, truly looking upon the world for the first time in decades. Gradually, bronzed flesh covered the muscle, dark hair grew upon their heads, and they were men again.

"So, I prophesied as He commanded me," Job said as the scripture came to an end, "and the breath came into them, and they lived, and stood upon their feet, an exceeding great army!"

The twelve Cherokee braves stood unsteadily for a moment, then grew strong and aware of their renewed condition. Contemptuously, they turned and regarded the one who had commanded them, but commanded them no more. Their fingers, fully-fleshed and white-knuckled with rage, tightened on their weapons as they started toward the fiend who had resurrected them.

With apprehension, Alkor Rank backed toward the dark portal in the air. "Such trickery has only delayed your reckoning," he told the two travelers. "If I don't end you, another will be sent in my place."

Dead-Eye ignored his threat. "You'd best get your bloody carcass back inside that hole and be gone, before they get hold of you."

The Bone Harvester had no human face to speak of, but even the crimson skull seemed less sinister in appearance and more fearful of what fate might befall it. With a defiant brandish of the bone scythe, Alkor Rank made his scorn clear toward them, then leapt through the dark doorway, returning to the fetid kingdom of which he had first mentioned.

They watched as the portal spun, its crackling border closing in, shrinking, growing tighter and tighter. Then, with a bullwhip crack, it was gone.

The Cherokee men turned their eyes toward Job, regarding him. Their stern faces, once rigid with anger and loathing, softened and grew uncertain. One by one, the weapons formed from the Harvester's magic and the minerals of the earth dropped from their hands. The deadly implements shattered and crumbled at their feet, then blew away as dust in the wind.

A strong, tall man stepped forward. He seemed unable to comprehend his present state or what it might lead to. "Now that we walk the Earth again, what must we do?" he asked in his native tongue.

The mojo man answered him, using the man's language to reply. "Find your wives, sons, and daughters, and live again. Farm, hunt, love, and grow old."

"It was a shameful travesty… a great wrong to our people… what your government did to us."

"True," Job told them. "And, believe me, if I had my way, their bones would be lying deep down in this earth, as dry and dead as yours once was. But that is beyond my power. So, all we can do is go on living and find purpose in it."

The Cherokee nodded in agreement. They bowed respectfully and then, together, the twelve started off across the prairie, in search of their people.

Dead-Eye reached to yank the spear from his shoulder, but the moment he touched it, it dissolved into dust and fell away. The same happened to the tomahawk. Bewildered by the turn of events, he swung down out of the saddle, retrieved his revolver, and began to attend to his horse. As he pulled the arrows of bone from Brimstone's body, the wounds flared with tongues of flame, then sealed over and healed with fresh skin and hide.

"You know," he said, looking over at Job, "we oughta find us a pulpit and lash it onto Balaam's haunches. Then you can set up and have preaching service whenever the mood comes upon you."

The negro flashed a gold and silver smile, but one of humility and not boastfulness. "Like I told you before, I use the tools appropriate for whatever situation presents itself."

"Nevertheless, if you choose to sermonize on a street corner in the next town we come upon, that's fine and dandy to me," Dead-Eye told him, swinging atop the Morgan again. "Afterwards, you can pass the hat for traveling money and I have no doubt whatsoever that the offering would be a plentiful one."

"I'll take that as a compliment," said the little man. "Now, let's get to riding and hope that no other delays befall us. Maybe we can get to N'awlins before Jules Holland and his gang depart and leave the trail cold again."

And, with that said, they headed south for the nations of the Creek and the Choctaw, and the border of Louisiana just beyond.

Chapter Nine

Black Bayou
East Louisiana
June 1867

By early summer they had left the flatlands of the country the Choctaw referred to as *okla humma,* or the "red people". The grassy expanse of the plains gave way to thickening vegetation—creeping kudzu and tall stands of cedar, sweet gum, and maple. As they left the farming communities and sugar groves behind, they found themselves entering the marshlands. Dark, shadowy channels of equally dark water topped with green algae, duckweed, and salvinia became more prevalent. Upon the dank shores of the swamp, and well into the still water itself, grew bald cypress, river birch, willow oak, and black tupelo. Heavy curtains of Spanish moss, gray and stringy, dangled from their limbs and branches, obscuring the sun and plunging the wetlands into gloom and shadow.

The further they traveled into the Atchafalaya Basin, the more troublesome and treacherous the journey became. Alligator and cottonmouth frequented the channels and venomous creatures such as coral snake, rattler, and copperhead infested the canebrake and clung to the branches of the cypress overhead. Several times a throaty hiss or brittle rattling would alert them of earthward peril and Brimstone would leap forward, crushing a serpent beneath his hooves before it had the opportunity to strike. In turn, the white mule grew bolder and less skittish. Several times, Balaam chased a young gator from the reeves and cattails along the marshy bank, but was sensible enough to leave the elder ones, or *vieillard*, as the Cajuns called them, alone.

As June passed into the sweltering, humid heat of July, Dead-Eye became convinced that they were lost in the tepid wilderness. Job was quick to quell those concerns, however. "I know these backwaters and canebrakes like the back of my hand. They are a part of me, as much so as my heart, mind, and soul. Once you are born and bred here, you are a part of it, no matter how far you stray."

They continued to follow the mojo man's lead and, eventually, came to the settlement of Breaux Bridge. The village was no more than a scattering of weathered, tin-roofed shacks along the waterway; a haven for trappers and poachers, and folks who had made their livings in the darkest recesses of the swampland, oblivious to the outside world. Many hadn't even known there had been a bloody war between North and South for four long, agonizing years, simply for the fact that it had never touched their part of the world

As Dead-Eye and Job rode through the town, the residents—French Cajun and Creole—went about their business and paid little attention to the two men. They were accustomed to strangers and transient travelers passing through on their way downriver to Baton Rouge or New Orleans.

They stopped at a mercantile near the dock to rest a spell and buy supplies. The proprietor was Arceneaux Maillard, a wiry, hawk-nosed man in his seventies with a patch over one eye and a gimpy leg, two inches shorter than the other. Job purchased coffee, cornmeal, fatback, and tobacco for pipe-smoking. He also haggled with the man on the price of a silver tea set that gathered dust on the shelf behind the counter. "Ammunition for the confrontation to come," the negro said after receiving a perplexed look from the gunslinger. "We'll melt it down for bullets, shotgun slugs, and such."

As the storekeeper took his payment, he appraised the little man in the derby hat. "Headed across de Black Bayou to Bogalusa Parish, are you not?"

Job was surprised, for there were a dozen settlements to pick and choose from along the bayou. "And how would you be knowing that?"

"Because I knew of your people," he told him. "Your father, Guelo, he was an islander from tropical places and your mother's name was Lucette… a slave girl who slipped de shackles and hid away in de swamps. Your name is Job and you are a *homme vaudou*… a practitioner of black arts and mysticism, but of a benevolent nature."

The black man seemed impressed. "My reputation precedes me, it seems."

"Indeed, it do! The battle fought between darkness and light at Bogalusa

Parish is legend hereabouts. Many folks, dey hold you in high regard, while only a few fear the powers dat you possess. Others are downright pissed dat you abandoned dem after such a hellacious ordeal."

"I have not returned to do harm or act as their nursemaid. Just came to acquire some things from my old homestead and be on my way. Do the Labarre Brothers still run their swamp boat across the bayou?"

"Dey do indeed," agreed Maillard. "And should be here within de hour, I would hazard to guess."

"Then we shall wait for them at the dock." And, with that, they bid the old man farewell and left the backwater store.

As they headed for the dock, Dead-Eye was curious. "These Labarre Brothers... who would they be?"

"Just a couple of ol' coon-assed Cajuns I know of," Job told him. "They possess the biggest pirogue in Louisiana."

Dead-Eye grinned. "Must make them mighty popular fellers with the ladies."

"A pirogue is a boat, smart ass. And they have one large enough to transport me, your flyblown carcass, and both our animals through Black Bayou to the Parish."

"What's so important about making this side trip? I thought we were headed to Orleans."

"And we most certainly will... after I retrieve a few articles from my shack near the Parish." Exasperated, Job removed his hat and wiped the sweat from his bald head with a red bandana. "Most dead folks lay there, all quiet and peaceful like. You gotta bitch and moan with each and every step you take." He appraised the man wearily. "Some folks down in the islands sew their zombies' mouths shut with needle and thread. Believe me, it's seeming more and more like a sensible practice, the more I ruminate about it."

As it turned out, they didn't have very long to wait at all.

A half hour after they had reached the Breaux Bridge dock, a boat appeared from the southern reaches of the bayou. Like Job had said, it was a big one, nearly as big as the flatboat Elias Caruthers and his eight strapping oarsmen had propelled across the bloody depths of the Mississippi. The only exception was that only two men commandeered this craft.

As the boat grew nearer, Dead-Eye studied the swampers. The one who manned the rudder was a small, dark-haired fellow, scarcely five feet in height, even shorter than the gunfighter Coltrane they had encountered back in the Ozark town of Blood Moon Ridge. The other—who single-handedly worked a long stave half as big as a telegraph pole—was a giant among men. He was albino and a good eight feet in height—even taller than the skeletal being named Alkor Rank had been—and was nearly half that wide at the shoulders. His head of hair was shaggy and snow white in color and his eyes were bright pink, the same as the white mule. The man's arms were massive. His wrists were as thick as fence posts and his hands large enough to swallow up a cannonball and nary a speck of iron show between his fingers. The gunfighter figured that the man would have no trouble at all pulling a man's head off his shoulders if he had the inclination.

Job noticed the gunfighter's interest and smiled. "Jorge and Lemuel... or Lemmy as he is called. They are twin brothers, born of the same birth sack. But something peculiar happened while they were in there. They would have likely ended up being normal-sized men, but Lemmy siphoned the health off his brother Jorge, and they came outta their mama, one abnormally large, the other a runt the size of a squirrel. Jorge has all the smarts and could talk an ornery bobcat into becoming a lap cat. Lemmy is simple-minded and like a boy of seven or eight years, but he's the strongest damned feller I ever did see. He's like Samson, Goliath, and Hercules rolled into a single man. Lemmy can have a fierce temper, too. If a man is foolish to bully or pick fun at him, he'll likely break every bone in his body. The same goes if someone treats his brother badly."

As the pirogue reached the dock, the little man looped a rope around the column of a piling and stepped onto the platform. A grin split his homely face when he saw the mojo man standing there. Most of his teeth were rotten or missing, and those that remained were stained brown with tobacco juice.

"Well, I do declare and kiss Mother Mary smack on the virgin lips! It's been a coon's age since we saw you last. Settling back in de Parish, are you?"

"Just a way-stop on a long and treacherous journey, Jorge," Job told him. "I was wondering if your services are available for a trip down to Bogalusa."

"You shall be getting it for sure, *mon ami*!" He eyed Dead-Eye with an arched brow. "Along with dis long, tall drink of poison well water and de horse and mule, I suppose?"

"If you believe Lemmy's back is up to pulling and pushing such a weight."

"Gah! Bêtise!" Jorge exclaimed. "My Lemmy, he would tote all four of you upon his back, waist-deep in quicksand, if I be telling him so! Now, come aboard and we be on our way."

As they boarded the flatbed pirogue, Lemmy caught sight of the little mojo man and a massive grin split his pale face. "Well, bonjour, Mr. Job! Boys, I ain't seen de likes of you in a long, long while!"

"It's good to see you, too, Lemmy. You been behaving yourself?"

The big man laughed. "Aw, I'se been good as gold, I have!" Suddenly, his eyes widened. "Dere's my friend! Dat mule dat looks like me, he does!" He rushed over and hugged Balaam tightly around the neck. The white mule tried to pull away, but Lemmy wasn't having it. Trying to break free was like trying to uproot an oak tree.

"Lemmy! Leave dat poor animal alone before you strangle him!" Jorge told him. "Pick up dat thar pole and shove off. Daylight's getting scarce and we've got us a long ways to go!"

Soon, the smaller Cajun had slipped the rope from the piling and the big albino was pushing them into the channel with barely any effort at all. The muscles of his massive arms flexed and rippled beneath the sleeves of his cotton shirt, looking on the point of tearing free of the seams.

And, so, they began their journey into the dark heart of Black Bayou.

An hour later, the open sky above the tree line on both sides began to dwindle and disappear as the upper branches of willow and cypress began to close in and intertwine. Soon, a dense ceiling of dark vegetation and great beards of hanging moss shut out most of the natural light. Although three hours still lay ahead of them until sunset, the gloom became so thick that Jorge lit a coal oil lamp to cast enough light to distinguish their surroundings.

Every now and then, they would pass long bars of sand and creek stone where the dark forms of alligators lay, their eyes glinting in the muted glow of the lantern. Seeing them seemed to excite Lemmy. "Look a dar at dem gators, Jorge! We're gonna wrestle dem gators someday, ain't we, Jorge?"

"Yessir, Lemmy," said Jorge, sitting at the tiller. In the lamp glow, a sad smile crossed his face. "We're gonna do that one a dees days."

"Lemmy has a thing about gators," Job told Dead-Eye softly. "Loves 'em more than anything. Like they were soft, cuddly rabbits instead of wet and scaly critters. Sometimes he'll flip 'em over and rub their bellies till they drift right off to sleep. The damnedest thing you ever did see!"

As they drifted deeper and deeper into the far, fetid reaches of Black Bayou, the churring of crickets and the peeping of toads ceased. A silence as thick as the humid summer air hung about them. Dead-Eye sensed that danger was about, unseen, perhaps watching them from the upper branches of the cypress trees or from the dark water beneath them, peeping from amid the algae and lily pads. Unsettled, he took the sawed-down twelve-gauge from beneath his coat and hung it on the horn of Brimstone's saddle, where it would be handy in the event of trouble.

"Have you seen him around as of late?" Job asked.

"Who?" countered Jorge. "Ol' Cat Daddy?"

"That's right."

Jorge arched his shoulders, as though a shiver had traveled down his spine. "It been a while, it has. But he's out dar, for sure."

"Who the hell is this Cat Daddy?" Dead-Eye wanted to know.

"An aberration, that's what," the mojo man replied. "Half-man, half-catfish. As far as I know, there's only one of him and thank the good Lord for that mercy. If folks leave him be, he'll gladly do the same. But if they come looking for him… well, there's no stopping him and no saving them."

Jorge nodded. "He be an ornery cuss, dat for sure! A couple years ago, I ferried a man through Black Bayou. A young man of high education and foreign breeding. Said he was a student of a man named Darwin who thought me and you were akin to apes way back. Haw! Do you believe that bullsheet? Anyhow, he came looking for Cat Daddy. Said that he had looked for a similar critter way down past Mexico along a river called the Amazon. Said there was a half-man, half-fish down yonder, too. A gill man is what he called him. But they never found him. Just tore their nets asunder and raised all kinda Hell.

"So, we took dat young feller into Black Bayou in search of Cat Daddy. Our voyage took us deep into places we should have never gone… probably dat no man had ever gone before. And we found Cat Daddy… or he found us. We anchored on Bergeron's Bar to camp for the night. It was like it was now… quiet as death with no bug nor frog daring to make itself known. We bedded down and, on about three o'clock in de morning, Lemmy and I awoke to a scream that would curl your toes! We looked over and saw a man kneeling over dat scholarly man… or what we thought to be a man. I lit de lantern quickly, I did, and thar he was. Cat Daddy in the flesh! Like a fish with a man's arms and legs, and a head broad and wide with gills opening and closing, and whiskers hanging low from its ugly face. And dem eyes! Cold, dark, and glassy… like it didn't give a squirting shit whether you lived or died.

"Well, I had me an old flintlock pistol and I touched it off at de critter. I know I hit it square between the blades of the shoulders, but it acted like it was no more than a skeeter bite! It leapt back into the dark waters of Black Bayou and was gone. When we got to dat poor feller, Lawd, thar was nothing to be done. Cat Daddy, he had done his damage and ripped that boy's face clean off the skull! We rushed him to Bogalusa Parish, but it be too late. He bled out afore we could even get within five mile of the place."

Dead-Eye appraised the dark water around them. "Tell me something... are we to be in the Parish soon, or have to camp for the night?"

"Oh, we got a far piece to go to Bogalusa," Jorge told him. "Dar will be no getting dar before morning. We'll have to dock somewheres and take our chance at some shut-eye, although it won't be a deep and restful one, for sure."

"My shanty is scarcely two miles ahead," Job told them. "We'll bed there for the night, behind locked doors, if need be."

Jorge Labarre nodded. "Dat sound right favorable to me, it do." He looked over at the albino giant who steadily poled them down the narrow channel of Black Bayou. "You hear dat, Lemmy. We be going to Job's abode. Prod that muddy bottom a sight faster and let's get dar afore midnight."

"Yes,um," was all that Lemmy said in reply. Then, with a mighty heave, the big man propelled the pirogue at a greater speed down the shadowy waterway.

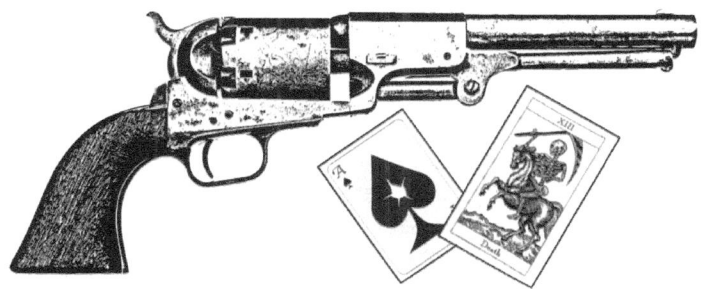

Chapter Ten

Job's Swamp Shanty
June 1867

It was well after dark when they approached the structure Job had once called home.

The shanty was weathered and sagging; its boards faded to a dull gray in color and the roof of sheet tin was infested with broad patches of orange rust. Half of the little house was constructed on the edge of a marshy bank, while the other half stood suspended over the dark waters of Black Bayou, supported by stilted pillions. A small dock had been constructed amid a tall stand of reeds, with a narrow set of steps leading to the building's front porch.

They expected it to be dark and forsaken. But, strangely enough, light shone from the shanty's front windows.

"I know you didn't leave a lantern burning for three years," Dead-Eye said.

"No sir, I didn't." Job turned to Jorge. "Pull up to that dock there and we'll take a look."

Jorge nodded to Lemmy and, soon, the flatbed pirogue was pulling up silently to the edge of the little dock.

"You want we should come with you?" offered the little Cajun.

"No, y'all stay put." Job pulled a pepperbox pistol from one of his vest pockets. "If there's a trespasser inside, I believe we can handle him." The negro looked over at the tall, mustachioed Southerner. Dead-Eye already had the big Dragoon revolver in his cold, dead hand.

"We're here if you have need of us," Jorge assured them. "Just give a holler and we be thar lickity split."

Quietly, the two crossed the rickety dock and mounted the stairs. When they reached the narrow porch, they crouched beside a window and peered through the dirty panes. A tall, stoop-shouldered man of dark-skinned heritage sat before a potbelly stove in the corner. His head—which possessed close-grown hair as white as snow—hung dejectedly, as though he had a world of trouble on his mind.

"Know who it is?" asked Dead-Eye.

Job studied the man hard. There was something about him that was vaguely disturbing, as though the squatter was someone he had once known from a very long time ago. "Perhaps. I won't know for sure until I stand face to face with him."

Soon, they had kicked the door open and stepped inside. The crisp *click-clack* of hammers being cocked filled the one-room shack.

"No sudden moves, mister," Job warned him. He aimed the pepperbox at the back of the man's wooly white head. "Now, slowly... turn around."

The man lifted his hands to his shoulders, then shifted on the stool he had been sitting on and revealed himself to the two.

The moment Job looked upon the elderly man's face, he knew who it was.

"Good God Almighty!" he exclaimed, allowing the pepperbox's joined barrels to sag until they were aimed at the dusty boards of the floor. "Papa? Is that you?"

The man stood and faced them. Job was shocked by the state that his father had degraded to. The last time he had seen the man named Guelo—before he had left briskly for a night of gambling and strong drink—he had been an imposing figure. Six foot four, as black as pitch tar, and full of vinegar and venom. His arms had been as thick and as hard as a cypress root, and his shoulders were squared arrogantly, as though daring any man to try him. But now, all of that was gone. Those magnificent shoulders were stooped with age and his arms had dwindled to willow branches. The dark skin that had gleamed in sun and moonlight was now dull and ashy. His eyes held no challenge, for all pride and pretentiousness had been beaten out of him long ago. They burned like a faltering ember— defeated, sorrowful, and full of regret.

"Yes, my son," he said. The deep rumbling voice had also suffered. It was scarcely more than a hoarse, rasping whisper. "It is I."

Job laid his pistol on an eating table nearby, then removed his hat and set it there as well. "This is... this is quite unexpected," he said, bewildered. "And damned disturbing."

"Is this the one you told me about?" Dead-Eye asked. He wasn't as trusting or as quick to holster his weapon. "Your father who disappeared in the swamp?"

"I am," Guelo said. He turned and regarded the tall Southerner with the bluish-white countenance. A small grin crooked the edges of his mouth, causing the wrinkles of his jaws and cheeks to dance. "Praise to Blanc Dani… is this your handywork, Job?"

The little mojo man nodded. "You taught me well, Papa."

"Indeed I did!" The old man walked slowly around the lanky frame of the gunfighter, examining him admiringly. "And a finer *zombi* I have never laid eyes on. And he talks? And thinks and moves of his own accord?"

"I do!" snapped the dead man. "I have no master. Especially not that sawed-off banty rooster boy of yours! And stop a-gawking at me or I'm liable to use this pistol on you, either as a club or how it was intended to be used."

Guelo frowned disapprovingly and looked over at his son. "Job… recall what I once told you? About sewing a zombie's mouth shut?"

Job nodded. "Don't think I haven't been tempted… and lately, too."

Dead-Eye scowled and returned the Colt to its holster. He walked across the single room of the little shack and stood with his back resting against the coarse boards of the wall.

"Sit down, Job," the old man requested. "We must talk."

He did as his papa said and, soon, they sat across the table from one another. There was an earthen jug of homemade shine sitting between them. Job swallowed dryly, then pulled the cork and took a long pull on the burning liquor. Afterward, Guelo did the same. Fortified, father and son began to converse.

"What happened, Papa?" Job asked after a long moment. "Where the hell have you been for the past forty years?"

With a trembling hand, Guelo reached into the pocket of his threadbare shirt and removed an object wrapped in white cloth. He laid it atop the table and, with fingers crooked and gnarled with arthritis, gently unwrapped the parcel. *"This,"* he said softly. "This is where I was."

Job's eyes nearly bugged from his skull when the object was finally revealed. "Impossible! You don't mean to tell me…!"

"That's right," Guelo told him solemnly. "The Stone of Kakudmi."

Dead-Eye left his place by the wall and grew nearer. It was an amulet affixed to a fine, golden chain interspaced with precious gems and black pearls. The talisman itself was oddly shaped, but beautiful. A pale blue stone in the shape of an hourglass, almost transparent in nature, with a peculiar inner glow in its center. The strange light ebbed and flowed, swirling like a dust devil on a dry and barren plain.

"Kakudmi?" asked the zombie. "What is that?"

"Not what," explained Job in wonder, "but *who*. There is an ancient poem written in Sanskrit called the *Mahabharata*. It was penned four hundred years or so before the birth of Christ. Legend has it that there was once a King named Kakudmi, who sought a suitable husband for his daughter, Revati. The two traveled many miles to seek council with their creator, the god Brahma. But, while in the god's plane of existence, they discovered that time moved differently in the heavens than on Earth. Before their visit had ended, millions of years had passed. Brahma betrothed the princess to Balarama, twin brother of the deity Krishna. As tribute to King Kakudmi, the god granted him a blue-stoned amulet that would return him to his own time. Kakudmi used it to rejoin his family and kingdom, while Revati stayed in Brahma's celestial realm to wed her omnipotent suitor."

Dead-Eye cocked an eyebrow and frowned. "Well, a wagonload worth of that tale went completely over my head, but I reckon there was some fascinating and enlightening point hidden amongst it somewhere."

Job reached out and carefully picked up the amulet. "Dammit, man! It's a gateway of sorts. A means with which to travel through time."

"Bullshit! There ain't no way anyone can…"

"I did!" Guelo proclaimed. There was a tone of anguish and regret in his quavering voice. "I sought this accursed juju for years! But when I finally found it—and put it to use—I wished that I had left well enough alone!"

Job studied the blue stone. The strange lights within the hourglass sparkled and pulsed. "How did you come by this, Papa? And why, in God's name, did you desire to possess it?"

"I had a dark and dangerous cancer inside me," the old man told him. "One called Hatred. I had harbored evil feelings toward a man back in the island of my birth… a devil named Johé! He was as black of heart as he was of flesh. He desired the woman I loved as a young man… my sweet Christelle Annoa! She scorned him and, merely to spite me, he raped and killed her. Heartbroken, I left Haiti, taking a ship to America. When I arrived, my bitterness had poisoned my soul and I became the vile and ungodly man that I was during the years of your childhood.

"Even as I loved your mother, Lucette, I still couldn't deny the pain of losing dear Christelle. I sought the Stone of Kakudmi, believing that I could return to the day before her violation and murder, and kill Johé instead. I heard that a man possessed the amulet—a rich plantation owner in Lafayette. I paid a man I knew—one without conscience or hesitation—to slay that man and bring the Stone back to me. He did as he was hired to do. He delivered it to me as I drank in the tavern at Abita Springs. By the time I left the place, it was midnight. I stumbled drunkenly into the swamp, until I reached the edge of a mossy bank. I unwrapped my prize, placed it around my neck, and focused on the hatred and rage that threatened to consume me. A brilliant light radiated from the Stone and engulfed me.

Before I knew what was taking place, it was as though I was shot from a cannon. I felt as though I was traveling at an alarming rate of speed… as though my very being was being torn from the moorings of my physical body!

"Suddenly, I found myself in Haiti again, on the streets of Port-au-Prince, near the place of my birth. It was no longer night, but broad daylight. Enraged, I ran to the home of my nemesis Johé! But when I got there, I found things not at all as I expected them to be. There was a young woman washing clothes in a scrub tub and a small boy scarcely two years of age playing in the yard of their *lakay*. I recognized the woman as Johé's mother, but thirty years younger in age. With horror, I realized that the *pitit* who played so joyfully in the grass was none other than my enemy! I could have walked up and snapped the baby's neck, but could not bring myself to do so. Frightened, I turned and ran. Some men in the city saw me fleeing and chased me, believing that I had committed some crime. I grabbed the Stone, wishing to be away from there. And, in the time that it takes a heart to beat three times, I was back in the bayou."

"If you returned to the place where you started, why didn't you come home?" asked Job.

"Because I wasn't in the same place in time!" Guelo told him. "True, I was in Black Bayou, but it was a swamp of a sort I was unaccustomed to. The vegetation was overgrown and grossly oversized. The ferns on the banks were as tall as I was and gators swam the dark waters, tenfold the size of Ma Gator or any other that resides here. I ran through the canebrake to my house, hoping to rejoin your mother… but the place was not there. I realized then that the bayou I now stood in was thousands, maybe *millions* of years young! So, I concentrated on the amulet once more… and, from that point onward, found myself propelled from one place in time to another, without conscious effort or control."

Prudently, the mojo man set the Stone of Kakudmi on the table top, aware of the power it truly possessed. "And for decades afterward you were lost in time?"

"For forty long years!" the Haitian moaned. "I have seen kingdoms and civilizations of the past rise and fall, and have dwelled in the distant future as well. A place both terrifying and wondrous at the same time, overrun with horseless wagons and great birds made of iron that filled the sky with thunder! It was enough to break me… to drive the arrogance and swagger of my youth from my soul and cause me to fear for my life, surviving day by day, hour by hour."

"I do declare!" said Dead-Eye, both disturbed and awe-stricken by the old man's tale.

Job laid his hand over the blue-stoned amulet and prepared to push it across the table to Guelo. Before he could, his father placed his gnarled and wrinkled hand atop his son's. "No," he said softly. "I am entrusting it to you, Job."

"*Me?*" The mojo man was hesitant to even touch it. "Why would I want the cursed thing? To suffer the same fate you did for all those lost years?"

"I cannot trust myself, son," Guelo said. "Deep down inside, I still harbor hatred for the one who violated and killed my Christelle Annoa. My fortitude shall weaken and I will most certainly go back to kill Johé… and my very existence will be laid to waste!"

"What do you mean?"

"During one of my many journeys through time, I came across an old man of Oriental blood. His name was Somchai and he knew the legend of the Stone and its properties, as well as its pitfalls. He warned me never to travel to the same lifetime in which I had lived. For, if I chanced to cross paths with myself and we looked upon one another's face, we would both cease to exist. Our shared existence would dissolve like sand in the wind and neither one of us would walk the Earth… or any other realm, be it Heaven or Hell."

"That's a grim thought," said the cadaverous gunfighter. "I'd say your best bet would be to take that damned thing and cast it, as far as you can, into the swamp yonder."

"No," said Job flatly. Carefully, he wrapped the Stone of Kakudmi in its cloth and deposited the charm into one of the numerous pockets of his vest.

"You're a bigger fool than I suspected," Dead-Eye told him. "You'll end up entangled in its sorcery to be ricocheted all over creation and beyond!'

"Someone must take responsibility to prevent it from falling into undeserving hands," the negro said solemnly. "And I reckon that someone is me."

"I'd not take on the task! It's disaster just aching to be untethered."

"You mind your guns and hunger for retribution," Job told him. His voice was soft, but stern. "I'll do what I feel is best. If I accept this talisman's guardianship, then so be it. It's my choice and my mortal fate, if its magic proves to be beyond my mastery."

Dead-Eye shook his head bitterly and threw up his pale hands in defeat. He walked away, knowing that further talk on his part was pointless. The little man had set his mind firmly to the duty and could not be swayed.

Job walked to the door of the swamp shanty and hollered down to the Labarre Brothers. "Y'all come and spend the night on the porch. You wouldn't want Ol' Cat Daddy to take hold of you. Or those dreaded swamp spiders—the *La Sanguinaire*—to wrap you in their web and feast upon your brains."

The speed with which Jorge and Lemmy grabbed the reigns of Brimstone and Balaam, and left the pirogue, was a testament to their belief in the dark and dangerous things of Black Bayou and their desire to avoid them.

Job turned and went to the center of the shanty floor. Taking the silver-bladed dagger from his sleeve, he pried at a board until it came loose with a squeal of dislodged nails. From the dusty depths underneath, he removed several objects—a lever-action Henry rifle with four boxes of brass cartridges, a leather satchel of potions and powders, and a drawstring tobacco pouch holding two hundred dollars in gold coin.

"What are you aiming to do with that?" his father asked.

"Take it with us on our journey," Job explained. "Dead-Eye has a vendetta to complete and I will accompany him every step of the way. For I have a wrong of my own that must be settled and put right."

"What sort of wrong?"

The mojo man's face was a mask of suffering and sorrow. "Your granddaughter," he told the old man. "My evil witch of a daughter... Evangeline. She is the wrong that must be dealt with and abolished." A grim expression filled his eyes. "And God help us all if she proves stronger of will and more adept in the ways of skullduggery and legerdemain than I am."

Chapter Eleven

Bogalusa Parish
June 1867

At first light the following morning, they prepared to depart for Bogalusa Parish.

The night before, Job had stoked the potbelly stove and melted down the silver tea set. He poured the liquid silver into the forty-four and thirty-eight-caliber molds, as well as molds for twelve-gauge shells and forty-four-forty rifle cartridges.

As Dead-Eye led the black Morgan and the snow-white mule onto the floor of the big pirogue, Job turned to his father. "I should hate and despise you for the way you were during my younger days," he told the man. "The countless times you betrayed my mother's trust in the bed of another woman or beat me until I could barely stand. But I harbor no such feelings toward you. In my way of thinking, you served your sentence and paid a harrowing price during the forty years that the Stone held you in bondage."

"Your forgiveness is not warranted," Guelo replied, "but I value it as an undue blessing. Thank you, my son."

"Stay here as long as you desire," the mojo man instructed. "Perhaps someday, when all is resolved concerning Jules Holland, Evangeline, and the others, I will show up on this doorstep once again. We shall spend our days drinking rotgut whiskey, playing poker, and fishing and trapping the length and width of Black Bayou. And the arcane business of hoodoo and its black magic shall no longer hold sway over our thoughts or actions."

Job shouldered the leather satchel and the Henry rifle and joined Dead-Eye and the others on the pirogue. As Lemmy propelled them back into the dark channel of Black Bayou, the little mojo man looked back and saw Guelo standing on the porch of the swamp shanty. The elderly man threw his hand up in a gesture of farewell and Job smiled and did the same. A melancholy feeling suddenly threatened to overtake him, for he couldn't help but wonder if that was the last time he would ever see his father alive.

"How long till we reach Bogalusa?" Dead-Eye asked him. The zombie leaned against the ramrod-straight frame of Brimstone, checking the loads in his forty-four Dragoon.

"Three hours," said Job. "Maybe a half hour more." He looked at the shadowy swamp that surrounded them. "I once took comfort in this place, but now I'm all-fired anxious to take leave of it."

"We'll get you to de Parish safe and sound," Jorge promised. "I vow and declare that to be the God's honest truth of it."

Job nodded. He believed the little Cajun, for the man had never given him reason to doubt or question his integrity or his abilities as an apt and able navigator of the dark channels and lagoons of the bayou. But something nagged at him, like a splinter that had burrowed into flesh and was hidden and inaccessible.

This swamp isn't done with us yet, he thought to himself. He took his pipe from a vest pocket, tamped tobacco into the bowl, and lit it with a sulfur match. *No sir! A wicked time still lies ahead. But what will it amount to?"*

He sat, cross-legged on the floor of the flatboat, smoking and contemplating why such a dismal mood should trouble him so.

It was nearly noon when they emerged from the dark depths of Black Bayou and entered the narrow channel of Bogue Lusa Creek, which led to the broad basin of Horseshoe Bay. As they crossed the lake-sized body of water, they could see the houses and buildings of the Parish ahead.

"Looks like we made it," said Dead-Eye.

"Dat we have," Jorge said with satisfaction. "I told you I'd get you here, now didn't I?"

Job left his meditation on the floor of the big pirogue and stood. He shielded his eyes from the glare of the sun and stared at the long pier that extended from the town's boatyard. A lone man stood there, as if waiting for them.

"Who is that yonder?" he asked.

Jorge Labarre left his seat near the rudder and regarded the one who awaited him. "I have no earthly inkling," he told them truthfully. "Never seen the likes of de feller before."

Dead-Eye walked to the bow of the boat and took a long, lingering look. "Aw hell," he said with a scowl on his pale-fleshed face. "It's John Legion."

The gunfighter and the mojo man exchanged a look of grim understanding. The demonic bounty hunter who Evangeline had hired to dispatch them had returned to finish the job. They had encountered him once before on a lonesome, country road near Dyersburg in Tennessee, and had come damn close to losing their souls to his serpentine shenanigans.

"Don't trick yourself into believing that this is over and done with," he had warned the two. *"Once I take a job, I don't rest easy 'til it's finished and the bounty is paid in full."*

Seeing him standing there, waiting for their arrival, they knew he hadn't been lying.

The tall, lean man with the long mane of raven-black hair was dressed in an ankle-length coat of equally black leather, as well as a low-crowned black hat garnished with a band of tiny golden skulls. His face was clean-shaven and handsome, but there was a dark gleam in his eyes that spoke of a malice and evil intent that mere words could not convey. The right sleeve of his coat had been cut away, revealing the bare arm underneath. It was elaborately tattooed from shoulder to fingertips to resemble a monstrous green viper. It was easy to surmise that the serpentine arm held the reserve of his power and magic.

"I told you I'd be back," he called out to them. "Now didn't I?"

Dead-Eye studied the man carefully. The double-holstered gun belt was strapped around his narrow hips as before, cradling the two oddly-shaped pistols that glowed a muted red, like irons hot and ready for branding. But the golden, four-barreled rifle he had sported before was absent.

"And we warned you of what we'd do if you ever set a loathsome foot in this realm again," Dead-Eye replied coldly. He turned his head and looked at Job. "Got that Henry handy?"

The mojo man tossed the repeating rifle to the gunfighter. The Southerner caught it in one hand and worked the lever, jacking a round into the breech. "Loaded with silver?"

Job nodded. "All sixteen cartridges. Freshly packed and ready for firing." During the War Between the States, the Henry had been known as "the rifle you could load on Sunday and shoot all week long."

Dead-Eye lifted the curved buttplate of the rifle to his shoulder and sighted down the long, blued barrel. He centered its sights on the breastbone of the one named Legion.

"Don't you think I learned anything from our last encounter?" asked the man with the snake tattoo. With a flowing sweep of his long coat, he unleashed something from the dark folds underneath. They took to the air and headed across the water, straight at those on the pirogue.

"It's those damned flying snakes again!" Dead-Eye gritted between his teeth. Working the trigger and level at an astounding speed, he fired six shots in quick succession. The rattlesnakes—deep violet in color with wings of pale green membrane—spun and swooped, their tail buttons rattling a brittle staccato. Their mouths opened wide as they intercepted each shot fired, swallowing the bullets whole. As the silver slugs entered their gullets and traveled the length of their bodies, they exploded into brilliant flashes of purple fire and filled the summer air with gray ash and sulfur.

"Well, I do declare!" said Jorge, startled. "What manner of belly-crawlers would dey be?"

"Not from dis swamp, I'd say," said Lemmy. The albino stood there, looking even paler in his face than he normally did.

"Not of this *time*," Dead-Eye muttered beneath his breath. He recalled how Legion had used the flying rattlers before, shooting them out the muzzles of his hellish rifle like poisonous projectiles. He also remembered the otherworldly bounty hunter boasting of them coming from a distant time known as the *Burn*. A time when "something infinitely more destructive than gunpowder could destroy cities and towns, forests and mountains, in the wink of an eye."

"So, is that all you have for us?" scoffed Job. His voice was bold, but his attention was wary and focused on every subtle expression on the man's face and each tiny flex of his muscles.

John Legion laughed. The sound seemed to take flight, filling the air like a flock of crows, thrumming through the hardness of their bones, tickling every nook and cranny of their brains. "No sir!" the bounty man replied. "I brought a leviathan with me. Something a bit more formidable… something that your petty charms and potions cannot devastate or defeat."

The four men on the pirogue watched as the man raised both his arms skyward. Abruptly, the white clouds that hung in the blue sky overhead darkened and grew black. Before long, the dark currents began to spin clockwise, like the funnel of a cyclone. But, strangely, there was no wind. The ebony gale was oddly silent as its center crackled with blue-white lightning.

Dead-Eye turned to Job. "What's he conjuring?"

The mojo man shook his head. "I have no idea… but whatever it is, it's liable to give us a helluva fight… if there's even a chance of us fighting it at all."

A great, deep-throated bellow sounded, as if from a distance. From the mouth of the funnel, a spray of fetid water erupted, stinking of rotten vegetation, decayed fish, and things from the deepest, darkest reaches of some hellish tributary... but not of the world that they knew.

The booming call of a great beast came again, this time close enough to cause the waters of Horseshoe Bay to churn and pitch violently. The two Cajuns, their passengers and their animals, fought to keep their foothold as the flatboat bucked beneath them.

Then, it was there. Coming through the portal, invading a realm it had never known... but loathed and despised, nevertheless.

They watched in horror as the beast—the thing John Legion called Leviathan—squirmed through the swirling opening amid the storm clouds, foot by foot, and yard by yard. It appeared to be a monstrous swamp gar, slender in form, its narrow body covered in thick, green slime and bulbous barnacles and swollen tumors. Its fins were massive, each the length of a railway car and tipped with spiny claws sharp enough to rend wood and stone effortlessly.

As it struck the lake's surface, a massive fountain of displaced water shot several hundred feet in the turbulent air. The creature reached the basin's muddy bottom, spun gracefully, and resurfaced with a mighty roar. That was when they saw its fiendish head clearly. It was the size of a locomotive, fifty feet or more from the base of its skull to the tip of its elongated snout. The beast's mouth opened widely, displaying row upon row of long, jagged yellow teeth, each as long as a man is tall. Decayed meat from some unfortunate prey dangled from the gaps between the fangs, and its breath stank like the visceral dregs of a lifetime of defeated and half-digested victims.

They stared into its narrow face, frozen to the spot, unable to move for a long moment. Its massive eyes—watery and gray– held no expression... or at least none that they could identify. But something emanated from the Leviathan... not sound, but a dark wave of dread and despair that seemed to assault them from within. It was the bone-chilling sensation of hopelessness, of the certain knowledge that their doom was imminent and that they would soon know the bitter vanquishment of death.

Dead-Eye was the only one who was not affected, for he was already dead. With a curse, he emptied the Henry rifle into the head of the swamp creature. Its dappled flesh seemed to absorb the silver slugs, leaving no evidence of scars or wounds. He tossed the lever-action to the side and drew his pistol. As the thing rose skyward, casting a dark shadow upon the pirogue and its occupants, he took careful aim and unloaded the forty-four into the flaccid folds of its throat. Again, the silver bullets did little or no damage. Whatever the creature was, it was not of a supernatural nature, but some abomination from some primeval world that the human mind could not possibly fathom.

Without warning, the giant gar dipped its monstrous head toward them, its jaws yawning wide. As it neared the boat, a long, serpentine tongue, black and barbed, lashed out and wrapped tightly around Jorge LaBarre's waist.

"Sacré bleu!" the little Cajun shrieked as he was hoisted off his feet, toward the toothy maw of the gar. "Dieu préserve mon âme!" Then, with a great gulp and a snap of its lengthy head, Jorge was devoured in a single bite.

"JORGE!" screamed Lemmy. He discarded his pole and, at a loping run, launched himself from the bow of the pirogue. The albino giant landed atop the narrow snout of the creature. He grabbed handholds of the beast's moist flesh, his fingers burrowing, tearing away fistfuls of fetid tissue and letting gouts of inky, black blood.

The monster wailed painfully, flailing its head to and fro, attempting to shake its offending parasite loose. Lemmy refused to let go, however. Slowly, he shimmied up the horrid snout, intending to reach the dome of the thing's skull. But, before he could reach the Leviathan's cranium and deliver blows that may have mortally wounded it, a massive fin lashed out. It scooped him up, tossed him skyward, and then swatted him like a spinster might swat a bothersome fly with a church fan. Lemmy spun, head over heels, above the little town of Bogalusa Parish, then crashed bodily through the roof of the rectory a quarter mile away.

With an ear-splitting bellow, the giant gar descended into the depths of the bay once again and was momentarily concealed from sight.

"What are we going to do to stop this thing?" Dead-Eye asked. He returned the Dragoon to its holster, aware that it was useless against the thing they confronted.

"I'm thinking on it!" Job snapped. He had the little book of spells and incantations open, attempting to find something that might do the trick. "Just give me a moment, will you?"

"I'm not certain that we have very many moments left!"

The surface of the bay began to churn and bubble turbulently as the creature prepared to emerge once again. But when it finally did, it appeared with a shrill cry of agony, flailing its grotesque head back and forth wildly.

"Look!" exclaimed Dead-Eye. "What the hell is that?"

They watched as something straddled the snake-like neck just behind the skull. At first, they thought it was a man, one every bit as big as Lemmy Labarre.

But then, they saw the creature for what it was. It had the form of a man, but its massive arms and legs were covered with dark, mud-slickened scales and edged with sharp fins along its forearms and the calves. Its clawed hands were webbed between its long fingers, and one of them had reached over a brow of the monster's eye socket and slashed viciously across the ball of the orb. A dark gelatinous substance shot from the punctured eye as the sack of the organ lost its firmness and grew flaccid.

It was the fish-man's head that was the most horrifying of its features. The skull was broad and mottled in patterns of black and gray. Its eyes were wide and iridescent in hue, with circular pupils, and at the corners of its massive mouth were long, fleshy whiskers, much like its much smaller counterparts who were plentiful in Bogalusa Bay, Black Bayou, and throughout the watery channels of Louisiana.

"It's Cat Daddy!" cried Job in astonishment. He had lived in the swamp all of his life, had heard the tall tales and legends since he was a small child, but had never laid eyes upon the creature… until that moment.

Half blind, the monster gar flailed its massive head, attempting to dislodge its attacker. But Cat Daddy wasn't about to let go. The other webbed claw descended and dispatched the other eye. The slender snout snapped blindly, its teeth gnashing one against the other, but finding nothing to sink its fangs into.

"Well, that sure didn't improve its mood any," Dead-Eye said. "I'm thinking the way it's bucking and thrashing, it might be more dangerous blind than not!"

"I'm thinking you're right," Job agreed. "If we don't do something soon, it could end up killing us and destroying most of the Parish, if not all of it!" The little mojo man fought to keep his balance as the flatboat pitched precariously back and forth. Suddenly, an expression of dawning inspiration dawned on his face. "Fetch the Staff from Balaam's pack! Quickly!"

Dead-Eye stumbled to where the white mule stood, legs splayed to keep upright. He dug through one of the canvas packs and withdrew the long staff with its tip fashioned into the head of a snake. He tossed it to the negro. "What are you going to do with it?"

"I'd say it's about time to call down a plague upon the head of this slimy son of a bitch!" Job told him. Then he closed his eyes and, taking the staff in both hands, raised it toward the heavens.

For a long moment, nothing happened. Then, gradually, a low droning sound drifted from the direction of the South. It grew in volume and intensity, until it drowned out the angry bellows of the Leviathan.

An instant later, a great cloud of buzzing, darting fury rolled across the horizon, moving above the treetops. Hungrily, the swarm descended toward the monstrous gar, unrelenting and unstoppable.

Cat Daddy seemed to sense what was coming. The fish-creature left its perch on the gar's neck and plunged beneath the waters of Horseshoe Bay, safely out of harm's way.

Then the pestilence engulfed the thrashing form of the gar—hundreds of thousands… biting, gnashing, stripping hide, muscle, sinew with ravenous fury.

"Well, I'll be damned!" said Dead-Eye. "Locusts!"

They watched, both fascinated and mortified, as the body of the Leviathan was stripped to the bare bone. Just as swiftly, they attacked and devoured its internal organs—entrails, lungs, heart, and brain—finally exciting through the empty pits of its eye sockets. Defeated, the monster crumbled and fell into disjointed fragments. As its denuded skeleton sank into the depths of the lagoon, the cloud of gluttonous insects took to the sky once again and was soon gone.

Dead-Eye looked toward the dock. John Legion stood there, not nearly as full of swagger as he had been before. A stricken look akin to fear crossed his handsome face. He turned and, with a circular motion of his hands, conjured the Hole Out of Nowhere to access a swift escape.

"Throw me that pepperbox!" the gunfighter called out.

Job shucked the little pistol from a vest pocket and tossed it to him. Dead-Eye cocked the block hammer, took steady aim, and fired.

A silver round ball was propelled from the conjoined barrels of the .36 pistol. It found its mark just as the crackling portal broadened and lengthened enough for the bounty hunter to squeeze through. The slug struck John Legion squarely in the left shoulder blade. The man howled painfully as the wound sputtered with sparks and flame and smoldered with sulfurous, black vapor. Then he was through the gateway and gone. A split second later, the portal was fully closed and was no longer visible.

"Do you think I ended him?" asked the gunfighter.

"I reckon we'll know if he doesn't trouble us again somewhere further down the trail," said Job. "But something tells me that he's a sight more tenacious than we believe him to be. Evangeline has offered him a bounty for our souls, and he aims to collect."

"We're still a hundred yards from the dock and with no boatmen to get us there. I reckon we'd better commence getting there."

Under Job's direction, both Brimstone and Balaam leapt into the water of the bay and began to swim to shore, lightening the pirogue's load. Dead-Eye took the oversized pole and, with much cussing and struggling, eventually pushed them to the edge of the pier.

When they stepped onto the boards, they found themselves surrounded by the townsfolk of Bogalusa Parish. Some seemed overjoyed to see the little mojo man, while others glared at him with contempt. A tall, severe man in a white collar and black cassock stepped forward. His face and body appeared to be all sharp edges and hard, rigid muscle. There seemed to be nothing soft or compassionate about him whatsoever.

"Father Bussiere," the mojo man said in acknowledgment.

"What have you brought for us this time, Job?" he asked in disdain.

"Salvation or damnation? You seem quite adept at providing both."

"If you'd laid witness to the spectacle, rather than cowering in your confessional, you'd know that I saved your holiness's righteous ass."

The priest scowled and regarded Dead-Eye. He suddenly recognized him for what he was, and his oversized hawk-bill of a nose flared at the smell of bodily decay. "Heaven help us all! What is this abomination?"

Job arched an eyebrow. "I'll thank you kindly not to be referring to my handiwork in such an offensive manner!"

"I'm the Lord's handiwork," the zombie spoke up. "You just left your fingerprints in the clay a little."

"Job!" someone called out excitedly. The negro looked past Bussiere and the others and was surprised to see Lemmy Labarre limping down the street toward him.

"Good God Almighty, boy! I thought you were dead, as far as that critter flung you!"

When the big man reached him, he saw that his pale face was bathed in tears. "What am I to do, Job? That *monstre*… it et poor Jorge! My brother… he did everything for me. Told how to do things and when. Woes! I'm doomed without him!"

Job considered the giant's dilemma for a moment. He took a gold coin from his vest and pressed it into the Cajun's massive palm. "I'll tell you what. You buy yourself a canoe—one big enough to fit you—and you head back through Black Bayou to my shanty. My papa… he is lonesome and in need of help, just like you. You can do for him and he'll do for you in return, just like Jorge did. You two can take the canoe back and get the pirogue and, together, you can ferry the bayou again. You pole and Papa can man the keel. How does that sound?"

"Do you think he'd do it?" Lemmy asked anxiously.

Job remembered the forlorn look on his father's face when they had left earlier that morning. "I know he would!"

The big man gathered Job in a crushing bearhug until the mojo man gasped for air. Then he walked over and shook Dead-Eye's hand vigorously, like he had hold of a pump handle and was attempting to draw water from a well. The gunfighter felt the stitches in his shoulder pull and creak with the strain. *Hell, there goes my confounded arm again!* he thought to himself.

Luckily, Lemmy stopped before the Southerner could lose a limb to the show of affection. Then he took the gold coin and headed down the dock to where pirogues, canoes, and row boats were sold.

"Are you not back for good, Job?" asked an elderly woman of Creole blood named Henriette Fontenot.

"No, ma'am, Miss Henriette. We intend to be on our way to N'awlins directly."

"But what if we are threatened again?" demanded a burly, bearded

Cajun named Pierre. "What if de demons you vanquished years before return… or some dire behemoth such as de one in de bay shows up to slay us? What shall we do then?"

"I know all of you think poorly of my papa, Guelo, but he has returned from a long journey, a changed man," the negro told them. "My advice to you? Befriend him and accept him as one of your own. His mastery of black magic and voodoo puts mine to shame. If you are loyal to him, I am certain that he will protect you from any menace that may befall Bogalusa Parish."

As the crowd began to disperse, Dead-Eye regarded his traveling companion. "It's scarcely noon," he told him. "I reckon we could burn seven more hours of daylight before bedding down for the night."

Job nodded. "I suppose we could very well reach Ponchatoula before the first wink of a firefly. Let's get to riding then."

As they mounted the white mule and the coal-black Morgan, the mojo man turned in his saddle. He surveyed the broad expanse of Horseshoe Bay as well as the shadowy entrance that led into the far reaches of Black Bayou just beyond. For an instant, he was certain that he saw something standing upon the bank—a tall, glistening figure that could have been a man, but more than likely was not. *Is that you, Cat Daddy?*

"What are you waiting for?" called Dead-Eye, who was already heading south for the marshland of the Delta and New Orleans just beyond.

Distracted, the mojo man regarded the gunfighter, then turned back toward the tall stand of water-logged cypress and the mossy bank that he had studied a moment before. The spot was empty.

With a grunt of resignation, Job reined Balaam to follow, knowing very well he might never lay eyes on the half-man, half-catfish again.

Chapter Twelve

Round Rock
East Texas
Late August 1867

A s it turned out, their trip to New Orleans had been a wasted one.
Upon their arrival to the gulf port city, Job visited a little shop in a dark alleyway off Decatur Street in the French Quarter, one with no sign out front and windows obscured with thick, black drapes. Only those who practiced voodoo and the black arts knew of the place or dared enter its doorway.

The proprietor, a free-born Creole woman by the name of Marie Laveau, greeted Job warmly, for both the mojo man and his father had been regular customers throughout the years. As she gathered a few supplies for Job—ground eggshell, mojo beans, raccoon pecker bones, and powdered mugwort and mandrake—the subject of Jules Holland came up. It turned out that they had stayed in the city for nearly two months, before departing and heading west for Texas in early April. It seemed that there was a clandestine society of Nosferatu in the city and, in their presence, Holland held a respect and standing akin to royalty. He had been too busy holding court in the crypts and catacombs of the Metairie to trouble the citizens of New Orleans.

"Evangeline, she was here a time or two," Laveau told him as she blessed and wrapped his parcels. "More to browse than to shop... and to make herself known." The woman in the white and crimson tignon chuckled, although there was a tone of contempt in her mirth. "The sorceress absolute, that daughter of yours considers herself. Arrayed from head to toe in black taffeta and lace, head held high like the queen sibyl. Oh, she is a formidable enchantress and powerful in the ways of necromancy, but the most potent of her magic is derived from the vexatious book that is in her possession. Take that from her grasp and she wouldn't be half the witch that her mère, Rosemonde, was."

As Job had reached to take his packages, Marie Laveau had reached out and touched his hand. "Take care, *chaman des marais!*" she had warned gravely. "I know you have Guelo's spell book, but the one she carries conjures evil and iniquity beyond our imagining. It holds keys to places no mortal man should have access to and beings that are best to remain unknown and confined to their own malevolent realms."

Before departing, Laveau had knelt before the shop's ritual altar, which was decorated with candles, tribute tapestries, and statuettes. She reverently lit incense of Nag Champa, myrrh, and patchouli, and prayed to the *vodou* priestess Les Lois for favor and protection upon Job and Dead-Eye during their pursuit of Holland, Evangeline, and the others.

For the next several weeks, the two traveled through western Louisiana, moving from New Iberia to Lafayette to Lake Charles. In mid-August, they crossed the border into east Texas.

Once again, they began to find evidence of the cruelty and turpitude that Holland and his unholy band was capable of. A small town called Nacogdoches had suffered grievously due to Evangeline's spiteful conjuring. According to a sheriff named J.R. Lansdale, a fiend had been unleashed from its nightmare realm, a horrifying deity clad in a top hat and mortician's coat who possessed a great fondness for shaving razors. After half the town's population had been slain or driven to insanity, the God of All Things Sharp had departed, but had vowed to return with a renewed appetite for destruction someday.

It was in the third week of the month of August that Dead-Eye and Job crossed a vast expanse of grassland and approached a small town upon the flattening horizon. As dark storm clouds rumbled and gathered overhead, they thought it best to seek shelter for the night. A weathered and barely-discernible sign at the side of the road marked the place as Round Rock.

Riding down the center of the dusty street, they came to realize that the place was completely deserted. The windows and doors of many of the buildings were boarded up and the main thoroughfare was littered with debris. From the amount of disrepair and neglect it looked as though the town had been abandoned for several years.

"What do you reckon happened here?" asked Dead-Eye.

"A boom town that came and went, more than likely," Job told him. "Cattle, I'd say. Beef on the hoof is many a man's livelihood in these parts."

"Well, it looks as though a few folks' trade went plumb belly-up." Lightning flashed in the distance, followed by the roll of thunder an instant later. "We'd best find a barn or such to bed the critters in and find us a dry hole to crawl into. There's a nasty storm coming in from the west and right fast."

Thankfully, the only two structures in the ghost town that were unboarded were the livery stable and the town saloon. As they sought out empty stalls in the gloom of the stable, they were surprised to find that one of the stalls was already occupied by a chestnut-brown mare. A Wade saddle, common among ranchers and cowhands, had been slung over the top of the stall gate until further needed.

"Looks like someone else had the same notion," mused Job.

Dead-Eye's hand fell across the curved butt of his Dragoon and absently caressed the ivory grips. "Wonder where they'd be?"

"No need to be going half-cocked," the mojo man advised. "Just 'cause we haven't seen 'em yet doesn't mean they're up to no good."

They shucked the saddles and packs off Brimstone and Balaam and left the two in a couple of empty stalls. Then they took their guns and saddlebags and headed next door to the saloon.

Halfway there, Dead-Eye stopped and studied the lavishly-painted sign above the porch awning. "The Long Pig Saloon. Odd name for a drinking establishment. I thought you said this was a cattle town?"

"Well, it could have very well been a hog town as well," said Job. The wind had grown in intensity since they had entered the livery and, looking toward the westward end of the long street, they could see a dense wall of rainfall a mile or so away. "Now let's get inside before we get caught in a gully-washer."

They mounted the rickety boardwalk and crossed to the front door. The double doors were partially open, but there was no sign of light within the structure, except for what shone through the two front windows. Cautiously, they stepped inside. Dead-Eye shucked the big forty-four from its cross draw holster and, thinking better of his initial warning, Job jacked a round into the breech of the Henry rifle in the event that trouble might show itself.

The saloon had once been a showplace, that was for sure. A long bar of elaborately-carved mahogany wood ran along the back wall and behind it hung broad mirrors—all cracked or shattered. Sturdy shelves that had once been well-stocked with all matter of liquor still sported a few dusty beer mugs and shot glasses. The wall was pocked with bullet holes and one slug had shattered the glass face of a German clock, rendering it useless. Near a staircase that led upstairs was a painting of a plump and naked woman reclining seductively on a red velvet divan, eating grapes. A dozen round tables with four chairs each sat around the boarded floor of the large barroom.

"Right elegant to be stuck out in the middle of nowhere," said Dead-Eye.

"That it was," came a voice from a dark corner of the room behind them. "An emporium of libation, games of chance, and soiled doves unlike any in this part of Texas territory. A shame that it offers nothing now... except for shelter for a trio of ol' saddle tramps such as us."

Dead-Eye tensed and shifted his shoulder a bit, as though intending on turning. He stopped when the metallic *click-clack* of a gun's hammer being cocked rang throughout the room. The former Confederate officer recognized the sound for what it was. "A Sharps falling-block, but not a carbine. More than likely one with a long barrel for long range shooting. Fifty-two-caliber, I'd say. The mechanism is loose and easy, so it's been put to plentiful use."

"It certainly has, both in war and on the plains. Just took leave from hunting buffalo to feed the railroad men of the Kansas Pacific. Me, William Cody, Bill Comstock, and a feller named Jefferson Gray brought down nearly four thousand head of the ornery beasts, for meat and hides, before I sickened of the slaughter and moved on."

"Very interesting conversation we're indulging in," Job said. "But I'd prefer to talk to you face to face."

"Then turn yourselves around... slowly."

They did as he instructed. Sitting alone at a corner table was a tall, rawboned man in a high-peaked hat and rain slicker. His face was leathery and tanned, sporting a broad, handlebar mustache and a sprig of chin whiskers. He sat with his boots propped on the edge of the saloon table. The heavy barrel of the big-bore Sharps rested upon one scuffed toe, aimed squarely at Dead-Eye's head.

"Name's Trampus Haines, originally of Springfield, Illinois. Hunter, cowboy, mule-skinner, and occasional deputy by trade. Sharpshooter for sure." He nodded to a bottle of whiskey sitting on the tabletop. "Drop aim on that gunmetal and we'll sit a spell and have a drink or two. I don't peg you for outlaws, although you look like you could split a gnat's ass at a hundred paces."

Dead-Eye holstered his Colt. "I reckon I could do such a thing, if I had a mind to," he said. "Although I've gotten downright accustomed to flies and bugs pestering my carcass lately."

Trampus raised his bushy brows in astonishment. "Well, I'll be damned. You are a dead one, ain't you?"

"That he is," said Job. He sat down at the table, poured a couple of fingers of the amber liquor into a dusty shot glass, and downed it with one swallow.

"I've heard tell of such before, but never seen it with my own eyes. Does it bother you any... walking and talking, when you should be playing harps and such near the Great White Throne?"

Dead-Eye eyed the little mojo man balefully. "It sort of ticked me off a mite at first, but I got over it. I assume that mare yonder in livery is yours."

"She is," the man replied. He nodded to Dead-Eye. "Sit and drink, partner. You're welcome to partake of your share."

"I'm not a drinking man," the zombie told him. "Nor an eating one, either."

The tall, mustachioed man shook his head, perplexed. "All the pleasures of living are lost to you, ain't they?"

"All but the need to do harm to those who have done harm to me," the gunfighter declared.

"Then I'm pleased to say I've not done a thing to earn such a distinction." Thunder rumbled overhead, followed by the gradual pelting of rain on the eaves outside. It wasn't half a minute later that the street outside was obscured from view by a driving downpour. "Given how it's carrying on in such a hellacious manner, we might just be holed up here for the night."

"More'n likely," said Dead-Eye standing at the saloon window, watching the steady rainfall.

"So, I'm thinking this was a prosperous cattle town at one time," said Job.

Trampus nodded. "It surely was. Round Rock was the hub of the wagon wheel for cattle dealings for miles around. I'd say four thousand head were driven in and bought and sold, in a week's time. Gold and beef exchanged hands and made many a rancher a rich man."

"And then it finally played out and dried up?"

"Not at all. Cattle is still king in these parts. That hasn't changed and probably never will."

"Then why did this town up and die?" the gunfighter asked.

A wry grin shown amid the bristles of the cowboy's mustache. "Because it's haunted."

Dead-Eye turned and rolled his one good eye. "Bullshit! Ghosts? No such things exist!"

"I'm right surprised that you'd disbelieve such a thing," said Trampus, "you pretty much being one yourself. A dead body with a living spirit trapped inside."

"Hmmm... never thought of it that way."

"He's pretty much on the money about that," said Job. "And, besides, you doubting and having seen the likes of vampires, werewolves, witches, and hellish creatures from other worlds along our journey? Your cynicism dumbfounds me!"

Dead-Eye brooded. "I reckon I'd have to see one to believe it."

"And, if we end up bedding down in this here saloon for the night, you'll have your chance," Trampus Haines told him. "'Cause the haint-in-charge resides within these very walls. That's why I'd prefer that this storm skedaddle and let me be on my way. From what I've heard tell, anyone who's ever stayed here from dusk to dawn was found dead the following day… their hair sapped of its color and their faces frozen solid in a rictus of fright!"

"What's the tale?" asked the little mojo man, pouring himself another swallow of red-eye. "I'm curious to know."

Trampus nodded and poured him another glassful, as if fortifying himself for the story to come. "The feller who owned the Long Pig Saloon was from somewheres up North… a man by the name of T.M. Clark. A big, boisterous soul eager to make his fortune serving liquor to cattle barons and cowboys alike. He had a parlor in the back for games of chance—poker, roulette, faro, dice, you name it. And there were ladies of questionable reputation in the rooms upstairs. All were as skinny as a hay rake and as homely as the ass-end of a mangy dog. And none too keen on their grooming and tub-soaking neither. Many a cowhand left with their pipes pumped and drained, but with a little something extra in the crotch of their britches as an unpleasant keepsake."

A brittle whipcrack of heavenly fury sounded overhead, as though setting the mood for the tale's completion. "Anyhow, Clark did well for a year or so, and the Long Pig became a sought-after haven for the weary and lonesome men who were without drink or female companionship whilst on the cattle trail for weeks at a time. Then, one night, a group of six rode into town. They were a rough bunch, suspected by many to be robbers of stagecoaches and banks from here to Ohio. The leader set to drinking and got shit-faced drunk. When T.M. Clark stood his ground and refused to serve him another swallow, the man, who claimed to have been a Union cavalryman, drew a saber from his side and hacked Ol' Clark's head clean off his shoulders with a single blow. When the patrons of the Long Pig rushed to the bar to apprehend the murderer, his men pulled their pistols and shot every one of them dead, even a couple of whores who were in the room entertaining. Then they rode out, never to be seen or heard from again."

"This feller with the sword," asked Dead-Eye with interest. "Did his name happen to be Garland Hughes?"

"Why, no," replied Trampus, puzzled. "It was Stapleton. Why do you ask?"

"Just some no-account bushwhacker that's stuck in Dead-Eye's craw,"

Job said. He regarded the lanky Southerner with skepticism. "I told you before, you ain't never gonna cross paths with that son of a bitch."

"I've been a-praying to the Lord about it," Dead-Eye told him. "If He hears my plea, He'll put him in my sights sometime or another."

"Can't say I believe that the Almighty even listens to the prayers of the dead. He's got a passel of living folks to contend with, pestering him with wishes and confessions, asking for miracles and forgiveness. Vengeance for a petty sin or two is likely a far piece down on his list."

Anger and contempt smoldered in the gunfighter's iron-gray eye. "Wasn't a petty thing for that boy and his mother," was all he said, before turning his gaze back on the rainfall outside.

"So," said Job, turning back to Trampus. "What happened after the massacre?"

"The townsfolk did the decent thing," Haines told him. "They hauled the bodies of those poor men to the cemetery on the edge of town… a field of stones called the Boneyard, for lack of a better name. They prayed over their gunshot bodies and filled in the graves, certain that was the end of it. But it wasn't. Soon afterward, every night at precisely midnight, T.M. Clark would come back to raise a ruckus, accompanied by all those cowhands, gamblers, gunfighters, and harlots who had fallen to the bullets of Stapleton and his outlaws. And until the first light of dawn, no living soul in town had a moment's peace. Doors and windows were opened and closed, things were flung and torn asunder, amid all manner of clamor and confusion. One of the spooks even took it upon himself to haunt the church and ring the steeple bell all night long.

"Despite the prayers of the town pastor and his congregation, those ornery ghosts refused to pull up stakes and pass over. The mayor even paid a Caddo shaman to do a tribal dance to drive them out of Round Rock. Nothing worked and, night after night, Clark and his ghostly patrons would show up, mighty pissed off and eager to raise hell for what had been done to them. The townsfolk endured their torture for a month or so, then decided to pack up and move to quieter, less rambunctious territory. By the fall of 1864, not a living soul was left and Round Rock became a ghost town… in the truest sense!"

"Looks like we'll have our chance to witness it for ourselves," Dead-Eye told them from the window. "For it doesn't look to be letting up… at least not until morning."

Job grinned and rubbed his hands together. "Well, now, this could prove to be a challenging evening indeed."

"You figuring to herd those asinine apparitions to the gates of Heaven… or Hell, whichever way they're destined to go."

A sly look crossed the negro's face. "Could be this was too much for a Bible-thumping preacher or a medicine man of native birth to handle, but perhaps some old-fashioned Louisiana hoodoo might be potent enough to turn the trick."

Dead-Eye and Trampus Haines regarded the little man... not with a skeptical eye, but with the realization that, if anyone could eradicate the doomed town of Round Rock of the phantom saloon owner and his immortal patrons, it might just be the one who sat drinking and contemplating the inevitable stroke of midnight.

Chapter Thirteen

The Long Pig Saloon
Late August 1867

It was well into the night when Dead-Eye sat reared back in a chair at one of the saloon tables. He dozed off a time or two, dreaming of things that had passed and things that were yet to come, but mostly he sat and stared into the darkness. Ripsaw snoring from Haines and Job competed with the crash and rumble of the storm overhead, assaulting the gunfighter's ears without ceasing. At one point, he nearly considered shooting the two sleeping men in order to provide himself with at least a bit of relief, then thought better of it. He'd lost much of his manners and tact in the event of his death, but hadn't reached the point of killing without provocation… at least not yet.

An hour passed, then another. Then a brittle crackle sounded and he lifted the brim of his hat a bit to peek out from beneath it. The big German wall clock caught his attention. The cracks in the glass began to heal themselves, followed by the circular opening of the bullet hole itself. He heard the inner gears and mechanisms of the timepiece begin to click and grind. Then the clock began to chime, counting off one strike of the hour after another.

Job grunted and sat up in his bedroll. "What the hell was that?" In turn, Trampus Haines gave out a groan and a fart, and sat up.

"I reckon y'all better wake up," suggested Dead-Eye. "Looks like the haunting is about to commence."

The two were on their stocking feet by the time the twelfth chime sounded. For a long moment, nothing happened. The storm outside, with its high winds, brutal rainfall, and crescendo of lightning and thunder, continued with no sign of ceasing. But the interior of the saloon was as still as those who stood in tense anticipation.

Then all Hell broke loose.

The glass mugs and whiskey glasses began to jitter and rattle on their shelves, then launched from their spots like iron balls shot from the barrel of a cannon. Several struck the gayly papered walls. They tunneled through plaster and shattered against the wooden studs beyond. Trampus and Job dodged and darted among the projectiles, cursing and crying out as objects struck them across the head and shoulders. A sawed-off axe handle—likely used for keeping unruly drunkards in line—spun, end over end, and clouted Job across the top of the skull. The mojo man dropped to his hands and knees in a daze, unable to find his bearings for a time. To avoid receiving similar treatment, the cowboy also dropped and hugged the floorboards.

Dead-Eye, however, stood his ground. A brass spittoon that sat at a corner of the bar's foot rail leapt up, spun across the room, and struck the dead man across the forehead. The rim of the cuspidor punched through pale flesh and bone, embedding in the dome of his skull. "Thunderation!" he exclaimed as he struggled to pull the urn loose. With some effort, he yanked it free with a sucking noise. When it did, a spurt of sluggish, black brains spilled from the wound and dibbled down his pale face from brow to chin.

The room was filled with a crescendo of sounds and voices, whoops and hollers, piano playing, gregarious laughter, and the sound of guns being fired. In the distance, the ringing of the church bell could be heard through the fury of the storm.

A couple of chairs floated from where they sat around a table, hung suspended for a long moment, then hurled toward the lanky gunfighter. Swiftly, Dead-Eye reached beneath his frock coat and swung the sawed-off twelve-gauge into line, cocking both hammers. The double blast obliterated the chairs before they could reach him, filling the stale air of the saloon with shards and splinters of wood.

The Southerner let the empty scattergun hang from its sling to his side and drew the big Dragoon from its holster. He felt foolish fighting barroom chairs, beer mugs, and spittoons. "Show yourselves, you ornery sons of the grave!" he yelled. "Or are you too cowardly to allow me to see you?"

The hell-raising noise abruptly ceased, as did the hail of objects and furnishings around the room. Dead-Eye stood poised, at the ready... although ready for what, he had no earthly idea. Suddenly, he felt resistance against the gun in his hand, as though something had taken firm hold. Icy fingerprints formed on the Colt's barrel and frost slowly formed on the curves and planes of the steel, eventually engulfing his right hand. He struggled to cock the hammer, but his thumb was frozen in place an inch from the spur.

"I think you've done gone and pissed somebody off." muttered Job. Weakly, he rose to his feet with the help of Trampus Haines.

"Y'all get upstairs!" the gunfighter told them. "Hopefully, they'll stay down here and keep me company for a while." Dead-Eye watched as the ice from the gun traveled up his wrist and forearm. Then, with a mighty laugh that echoed more in his mind than his ears, he watched as the specter that confronted him began to materialize.

It was a big man in a white cotton shirt, red sleeve garters, and a black bowtie, dressed like most men who waited bar and served drinks to paying customers. But a couple things about him distinguished him from a living, breathing being. First of all, he emitted a ghostly blue aura around him, one that cast an icy coldness.

And, secondly, he possessed no head whatsoever.

"Jumping Jezebel on a jackrabbit!" exclaimed Trampus from the staircase. Both he and Job witnessed the ghost that confronted the zombie gunman with a mixture of astonishment and horror.

"I said, get your asses upstairs!"

As the two reached the second floor, Dead-Eye felt the freezing temperature increase around him and, abruptly, he was lifted several inches off the saloon floor. He hung there for a long moment, struggling to break free. Then, abruptly, his lanky frame was hurled forcefully across the room. He spun, head over heels, and crashed into a wall between two side windows. With a grunt, he slid to the floor and sat there, addled. As his head began to clear, he saw that the headless ghost was accompanied by a dozen or so others. All looked to be bloody and gunshot, and all possessed the same eerie glow as their otherworldly leader did.

As they advanced toward him, the gunfighter looked for some way to stop them, well aware that shooting at them would do no good. Then the clock on the wall behind the bar caught his attention. The glass and the face of the timepiece had healed at the stroke of midnight and, now, the ornate hands spun swiftly clockwise, speeding past one Roman numeral after another.

Without a second thought, he bashed his gun hand against the leg of a nearby table, shattering the ice from both his fingers and the pistol. He fanned the hammer, sending six slugs into the clock on the wall. Soon, the glass, face, spinning hands, and the inner workings of the timepiece were utterly destroyed. And, almost as quickly, the ethereal beings halted their advance and vanished from sight.

Well, I'll be damned, he thought to himself as he stood and cleared the brains from his face with the back of his hand. He took a handkerchief from his coat pocket and stuffed it into the hole in his skull; a temporary fix until Job could manage to repair the damage. *I had absolutely no notion that was gonna work!*

He surveyed the barroom. It looked exactly as it had the first moment they walked in—dusty and abandoned—except for the remains of the gunshot clock, the broken chairs, and other debris from the ghost attack. He listened and knew that the threat hadn't been obliterated. The church bell still rang continuously in the dead of night and, in the street, there were ghostly gunshots and hell-raising.

"Is it alright to come down now?" hollered Trampus Haines from the top of the stairs.

"It is," the gunfighter assured them. "For the time being."

The two descended the stairs and joined Dead-Eye beside the mahogany bar. "What in tarnation did you do to scare them off?" Job asked. He steadied himself and probed at the tender spot on his scalp.

The zombie shrugged his narrow shoulders. "I just saw that clock on the wall spinning like a runaway wagon wheel and I shot the hell out of it. Not sure why it had such an effect, but glad that it vexed them enough to light out. At least for a while."

"I'm thinking these spirits are stuck in a point in time," the mojo man pondered. "Between the moment they died and the moment they were laid to rest. Except it's clear to see they ain't resting properly. They're spiritually attached to the one that served them so much joy and pleasure in life."

"T.M. Clark," said Trampus.

"Yes." A puzzled expression crossed the mojo man's face. "Was I simply addled by that clout on the noggin, or was his spirit headless?"

"That he was," agreed Dead-Eye. "Right down to the collarbone."

"I know a thing or two concerning ghosts and their ways of haunting. And it seems to me that this one—this saloon owner named Clark—is particularly tempestuous in death on account he's missing his head. More than likely, he refuses to move onward because he was buried without it."

"So, you're saying when Stapleton decapitated the feller, his head rolled off somewhere and was forgotten?" asked the gunfighter.

"That's right," said Job. "And if we're aiming to settle this nightly ruckus and herd these boisterous bastards toward the great hereafter, it's up to us to find it."

Chapter Fourteen

The Boneyard
Late August 1867

Alll three looked around the downstairs room of the saloon. Their eyes settled on the long bar of intricately-carved mahogany.

"Did Clark have a barkeep?" Job asked.

"Not that I know of," replied Trampus. "He did all of the serving. Didn't trust anyone around his liquor but himself."

"So, he would have been standing yonder behind the bar when Stafford laid the blade to him."

"Yes, I'd say so."

Spryly, the little mojo man climbed atop the dusty surface of the counter and hopped down to the other side. He examined the floor, then raked away a thick coating of dust with the sole of his shoe. Soon, he discovered a broad oval of dried blood upon the floorboards. "Here's where he gave up the ghost... so to speak." The negro examined the length and breadth of the narrow aisle between the wall of shelves and the back of the bar. Suddenly, at the far end, something caught his eye. It was an open trapdoor, roughly three by three feet in width and depth. Within the portal was a veil of cobwebs with only pitch darkness beyond. "Where do you suppose this goes?"

The saddle tramp leaned over the counter and took a look. "Most saloons store their beer and whiskey in kegs in the cellar. They have a trapdoor behind the bar, so someone can lift a keg up to them through the hole when they need it. I suspect that is what this is."

Job displaced more dust with the toe of his boot and found a blood trail leading from the oval stain to the open portal. "Well, that's where his head went. When it hit the floor, it rolled right into that hole like a billiard ball into the corner pocket." He grimaced as he stared into the darkness. "Could be spiders down there. Maybe rats."

"Aw, hell!" grumbled Dead-Eye. "I'll go fetch it. A few spiders ain't gonna make much difference to me. They can set up house in my carcass and keep the maggots company, if they so choose."

"Must be a genuine pleasure traveling with him," said Trampus Haines.

"A blessing each and every day," Job told him wearily.

Dead-Eye looked around for a door that led to the basement and spotted one beneath the staircase that led to the second floor. He opened the door and looked down into the gloom.

"Want I should light you a candle or such?" asked the mojo man.

The dead man pointed to the eye that had been blinded with raw foxfire. "I should be able to find my way around just fine."

"Best get down there and find it," Trampus suggested. "You kind of startled those ghosts when you shot that clock, but I suspect they'll be coming back soon. Pissed off, more than likely."

"I'm a-going," said Dead-Eye. Then, with the yellow glow of his left eye illuminating the way, he descended the wooden stairs to the cellar below.

When he reached the bottom, his eye cast a pale glow a yard or so ahead of him. Wooden barrels and crates of bottled whiskey and rum lined the walls. The gunfighter started across the earthen floor and almost immediately saw what he was looking for.

The decapitated head of T.M. Clark sat alone in the far corner. He had expected a naked skull, but it wasn't like that at all. Sunken, dried skin clung tightly to the bone and there was still a little fringe of wispy hair around the ears and back; apparently the saloon owner had been a bit sparse on the top. There were no eyes to speak of, only empty sockets, as though the orbs had rotted away or had been eaten by some varmint. The lips were missing, too. The man's teeth grinned hideously from the head's place on the cellar floor.

With a sigh, Dead-Eye walked over to retrieve it. *Hellfire and damnation!* he thought to himself. *I always get the shitty chores.*

He was almost to the head, when a cloying odor assaulted his nostrils. A mixture of French perfume and putrid, rotten flesh.

"Well, who do we have here?" a feminine voice mused behind him. The tone was coarse and husky, like someone who smoked tobacco as much as they breathed fresh air.

For a moment, an uncomfortable memory came to his mind. His wife, Elizabeth, in the cellar of their mansion back home—pale, undead, and hungry for fresh blood.

"Looks like a long, tall handsome feller to me," said another, sultry and playful-like. "And he's dead, to boot!"

He turned to see a couple of women standing behind him. They were dressed in black corsets and frilly bloomers, and one wore a hat with an ostrich plume on top. The redhead was sporting half a face; the other side had been blown away by a shotgun blast or such. The other woman, a brunette, was riddled with bullet holes. Both stank like a fish market next to a slaughterhouse on a hot July afternoon.

Dead-Eye shook his head and started toward the far corner of the cellar again. "Whores," he mumbled beneath his breath.

"What are you slunking around down here for, sugar plum?" asked the redhead.

"Came to fetch your boss man," he told her. He stooped down and grabbed the decayed head, sticking his fingers in the eye sockets for a good handhold.

The brunette's bullet-pocked face pouted up. "Right disrespectful, the way you're handling poor Toddy-Woddy."

Dead-Eye looked at the head in his hand. It grinned up at him, as if in eternal amusement. "Was that his name?"

"Toddeous Miles Clark," the redhead said proudly. "But to us, he was our dear, sweet Toddy."

"Sounds right fancified, to me. No wonder he preferred to stick with the T.M." He took a couple of steps toward the stairs, but two saloon girls blocked his way. "What are y'all doing down here anyway? Don't you want to cavort and raise hell with the fellers upstairs?"

"We're down here to be with our honey-dumpling," said the brunette. "Of course, he ain't as fun or pleasurable as he once was. You don't get much poking and prodding from no more than a head."

The redhead with the ostrich-plume hat walked up and ran her bony hands along the Southerner's shoulders. "But now that you're here... you wanna roll in the sheets a time or two with Ol' Fanny?" She nodded suggestively toward a far corner of the basement. There, where there had been nothing before, was a large brass bed with velvet pillows, glowing an eerie blue.

"That there bed ain't real," Dead-Eye told her flatly.

"It is for us!" snapped the dark-haired girl.

"Well, I reckon a ghost bed would work well for ghost whores. But I'm still in an earthly body, so I'm certain that it'd not support me in the way its intended to. Besides, I'd just soon rut with a dead dog in a ditch than you two."

"Did you hear that, Mable?" exclaimed Fanny. "High-falutin, uppity zombie! With your undertaker's suit and shit-bucket hat! Think you're better than us?"

"No, ma'am. I *know* I'm better. And I'll thank you to not be disrespecting my duds in such a manner. As far as I recollect, no one has ever shit in my hat."

Fanny moved to drop her drawers. "I'll gladly oblige you in that respect, you high-stepping dandy!"

"You'll do nothing of the sort! There will be no glowing turds upon my head. Now step aside!"

"What the hell are you doing down there?" called Job from the trapdoor. "Who are you talking to?"

"I'm contending with ghostly whores!" he yelled back.

"Well, button your britches and get that skull bone up here. There's no time to waste!"

Dead-Eye was hurt that Job would even think him capable of such a thing. "Next time, you can go down and fetch your own severed head! Even if there are spiders about... which I doubt, since I haven't laid eyes on a single one."

"Oh, they're here alright!" said Fanny. She grinned broadly and a nest of black widows and fiddleback spiders began to skuttle from the cave of her ruined face.

Dead-Eye refrained with distaste. "I'd have taken your word for it, lady. No need to bring 'em forth for my sake."

"Aw, let him pass," said Mable contemptuously. "He was right cute at first, but he's a trying one on the nerves, he is!"

"You gonna leave Toddy here with us?" asked Fanny hopefully.

"Afraid not," Dead-Eye told her. "He's bound for the grave as he already should have been. You oughta go, too. I'm sure you've got a couple of plots reserved in the trollop section of the cemetery."

"But it's hot out yonder!" moaned Mable petulantly. "Not a shade tree to be found."

"It's nice and cool down here," said Fanny. "And the menfolk ain't pawing and panting all the live-long day."

"Suit yourselves." He mounted the stairs and, allowing the glow of his eye to light the way, joined the others upstairs.

"Now, what was that about whores?" asked Trampus.

Before the gunfighter could answer, the church bell began to ring in the distance, as well as the reports of a few phantom gunshots. "They're starting it up again." Dead-Eye started to toss T.M. Clark's recently-recovered head to the mojo man.

"No! You're doing a fine job holding it for me," Job told him. He turned to Trampus Haines. "You say this Boneyard is located on the far side of town?"

Through the windows they could see the transparent, blue forms of ghosts running up and down the street. "That's right. But it's a far piece to walk. We'd best saddle the animals and ride. If what you plan on doing ends up working, I intend on hightailing it away from here soon afterward. Half a night in this blasted town is enough, even without a passel of spirits to pester you."

Job nodded. "A right sensible idea. We'll probably do likewise."

Then, as the commotion on Round Rock's main street grew louder and more boisterous, they exited through the gambling hall behind the barroom and out the back door.

Ten minutes later, the double doors of the livery stable burst open and the three men and their mounts rode into the center of the street.

"Lord have mercy!" exclaimed Trampus. "Will you look at this here!"

There seemed to be three times as many ghosts as there had been in the saloon earlier. It looked as though T.M. Clark had recruited the entire population of the Boneyard to assist with his haunting. Many fired rifles and pistols, in the air and at one another, while half a dozen or so were having a hellacious brawl in the street. They even saw a big-boned woman in a bonnet and calico dress bashing the brains out of an unfortunate husband, again and again and again, with a stick of firewood.

As they reined toward the western end of town, they heard the distant rumbling of hooves upon hard-packed earth. They looked eastward and saw a stampede of skeletal cows and steers heading straight for them. Several of the murdered saloon patrons rode equally bony horses, firing guns to drive the herd onward. Leading the procession was the headless specter of the saloon owner driving a wagon full of soiled doves. The harlots were haggard and in various degrees of decay, firing single-shot derringers and cackling uproariously.

"Sweet Jesus on a Judas jackass!" exclaimed Dead-Eye. "More ghost whores!" He saw Fanny and Mable sitting amongst the harem, grinning seductively and waving at him. "Let's get to the graveyard and get that head planted… pronto!"

They took off at a gallop, spurring their mounts and gaining speed. The angry apparitions kept pace as Clark cracked a ghostly bullwhip, driving the wagon team onward.

Job looked over his shoulder once and was alarmed to see that there was scarcely sixty feet between them and the advancing army of spooks. "Throw coal to the flame, boys! I smell cow shit and filthy bloomers!"

When the weathered picket fence of the Boneyard was visible a ways up ahead, Dead-Eye felt Brimstone grow hotter and hotter beneath him. The black Morgan snorted ferociously, sending sparks shooting from his flared nostrils. "Y'all head on to the cemetery," he hollered, tossing the mummified head to Trampus Haines. "I think Ol' Brimstone has had his fill of running."

As the two men continued toward the end of town, the gunfighter reined his horse sharply around. Brimstone faced the approaching apparitions, his eyes as red and hot as the grate of a runaway locomotive. He dug his hooves into the muddy earth of the street and stood his ground, as the wave of ill-tempered haints barreled toward them at breakneck speed.

They were no more than twenty feet away when the demon-steed opened his mouth and unleashed an ear-splitting bellow like the shrieks of a thousand damned souls. A tongue of flame shot from his gullet as red and blistering as hellfire, expanding rapidly, blocking their progress. When the explosion of internal Armageddon dissipated, Dead-Eye discovered that the ghosts had, too. The church bell continued to ring, but Clark and his phantom posse had fled for the time being.

By the time Dead-Eye reached the Boneyard, Job and Trampus were already off their mounts and searching for the grave of T.M. Clark.

"Over here!" called the mojo man.

Dead-Eye shucked a shovel and pick they had found in the livery stable from one of Balaam's canvas packs. When he reached the grave, he tossed the pick to the lanky cowboy. Trampus set the decomposed head atop a tombstone and commenced to breaking earth. The marble marker read T.M. CLARK—BORN 1812–DIED 1862. CUT DOWN AT THE HEIGHT OF HIS POPULARITY & SUCCESS. REQUIESCAT IN PACE.

"*Pace*, my rotten ass!" spat Dead-Eye as he began to dig. "More like *tristitia*, if you ask me!"

Despite the desperation of the moment, Job was impressed. "Hell! I didn't know you spoke Latin!"

"I told you before… I'm an educated man."

Suddenly, the ringing of the church bell began increase. The volume and reverberation of the noise rolled through the graveyard with such ferocity that the sound thrummed through their bones. They looked toward the buildings of Round Rock and saw a vast dome of ethereal blue light above the peaks of the structures. Without a doubt, it was definitely a ghost town in the truest sense of the term.

"Dig faster!" urged Job. "I've got a feeling in my bones that we may be joining them if we don't take care of this matter in a hurry."

"We're digging as fast as we can!" said Trampus.

A minute hadn't passed, when the steel of Dead-Eye's spade scrapped coarsely against something. "I've hit wood!"

Soon, they had the lid of the pinewood casket lid cleared. Trampus pried at the edges with the edge of the pickaxe until the nails pulled loose with a squeal. The cowboy placed his weight against the hickory handle and, with a wrench and a grunt, popped the cover free. As he and Dead-Eye climbed out of the open grave, Job jumped in, flung the lid aside, and straddled the emaciated corpse of T.M. Clark. Just as they had suspected, the saloon proprietor had been buried without his head.

"Toss it down to me!" the mojo man requested. "And be quick about it!"

Trampus Haines moved toward the tombstone to grab the head, when he looked toward the cadaverous gunfighter and froze. "Dead-Eye! Behind you!"

The zombie whirled on his heels to find the glowing apparition of the murdered saloon owner standing directly behind him. Before he could react, T.W. Clark took a couple of steps forward and merged with the gunfighter's earthly body. Dead-Eye felt an icy coldness engulf him, within and without. "The ghostly bastard is inside me!" he cried out, more in warning than fear.

Job and Trampus watched as Dead-Eye shuddered violently, his muscles tensing, the dead tendons stretching and creaking like old leather. Both his eyes, good and blind, rolled up into his head. Then, when they slowly lowered to their proper alignment, the gunfighter's face took on an uncustomary expression of smug malice and cruelty.

"You should have rode on and not meddled in affairs that didn't concern you," he said in a crisp, Northern voice that was not his own. Then with a triumphant grin, he drew the big Colt from its holster and, extending it at arm's length, cocked the hammer. He centered the pistol's sight on the center of Job's startled face.

"What's happening?" Trampus asked, confused by the turn of events.

"He's been possessed, that's what." Despite his usual bravado, the mojo man's eyes were fearful and uncertain. He stared the long, tall gunman in the face. "Dead-Eye... son," he said softly. There was almost an edge of pleading in his tone. "Please... don't."

"Don't worry," the voice of Dead-Eye declared, struggling past lips that no longer felt in his ownership. "It ain't gonna happen!"

"Oh, I don't know about that," said Clark from inside him. "You're not as strong as you think you are. I pulled up stakes and rode all the way to Texas to find my fortune, then died scarcely two years later. Seems that I've got a second chance owed me. I'll just keep this body of yours, as putrid and broken-down as it is, and start all over again."

There was a clank from the right as the pick hit rocky earth. The gunfighter turned in time to see Trampus Haines drawing a Colt Navy from its side holster. The big Dragoon shifted its aim and boomed loudly. A forty-four slug skinned the hide off the cowboy's middle knuckle and plowed a furrow all the way up his forearm to his elbow. With a yelp, Trampus dropped his pistol and clutched his injured arm.

The ghost smiled cruelly with the cold, dead muscles of the Southerner's lean face. He turned his aim back to Job, held it there, and cocked the hammer. "Now, where were we?"

"Get the hell outta my head!" warned Dead-Eye. The muscles of his gun hand twitched and grew rigid, attempting to alter the direction of the muzzle.

T.M. Clark laughed. "No, I don't believe so." He corrected his aim and prepared to fire. "You should have left well enough alone, you meddling, little—"

"I said... GET OUT OF MY HEAD, YOU WHISKEY-SOAKED, WHORE-HUMPING, YANKEE SON OF A BITCH!" And, with that, Dead-Eye wrestled control of himself. Without hesitation, he inverted the six-shooter, jammed the muzzle of the forty-four under his nose, and pulled the trigger.

Brains, hair, and fragments of skull burst through a hole in the crown of his hat. The act was so unexpected that the spirit that dominated him was driven out. Job and Trampus watched as the blue specter separated from Dead-Eye's flesh and blood body and staggered backward, stunned and confused.

"Trampus!" Job yelled out.

With his uninjured hand, Haines batted the skull off the top of the tombstone. It dropped into the mojo man's dark hands, pretty as you please. An instant later, Job crouched and jammed the head directly upon the shaft of the severed neckbone.

The addled ghost staggered about for a moment, then his form shimmied like heat waves off a hot stone. They watched as he grew twelve inches taller in height. An expression of perplexity crossed his broad, mustachioed face as he lifted his hands and felt of his newly-reunited head.

"Well, I'll be damned!" he muttered in amazement.

"Considering the piss-poor way you treated us," said Job, "more than likely!"

"My apologies, gentlemen," he said sadly as he began to fade from sight. "I wasn't entirely myself." Then, an instant later, he was gone.

An expression of weary relief crossed Job's face. "That was just too damn close for my liking." He regarded the zombie gunslinger. "Good thing you derailed that barkeep's plans before he could pull the trigger."

Dead-Eye grinned wryly. His face was a bit lopsided and distorted from the force of the self-inflicted gunshot. "I don't put a bullet in my head for just anyone, you know."

The mojo man smiled. "Much obliged."

A low, mournful howling reached their ears. They looked in the direction of town and saw that the peculiar blue halo over the town was gradually ebbing in intensity. The sounds of gunshots, hoofbeats, and hooting and hollering abruptly grew quiet. The last thing that ceased to be was the monotonous ringing of the church bell. Then, it too, grew silent.

From where they stood, the streets looked dark and empty, and the buildings and houses utterly abandoned. It appeared that the hold T.M. Clark had over the spirits of the Texas cattle town had been broken and they had been set free. All the ghosts had gone out of the ghost town, leaving only an empty shell of a place called Round Rock.

"Well, I don't know about you fellers, but I'm not sticking around here a single moment longer," said Trampus Haines. "I'm heading down to Austin like I first intended. Got a job waiting for me there, busting broncs and branding calves."

Seeing that he was having difficulty mounting his horse with his injured arm, Dead-Eye walked over and gave him a hand. "Sorry if I crippled you. Clark was aiming for your heart, but I managed to alter his aim a few inches to the left."

"I do appreciate that," said Haines. He grimaced as he flexed the fingers of his right hand. "Looks to be in fair working order. I've heard tell that a doctor has hung his shingle at Wells Branch. I'll seek him out and have him attend to it. In a week or so, it'll be back to its old card-dealing, bottle-lifting self again."

They bid him farewell and watched as he headed south on the chestnut mare.

Having nothing more to keep them there, the gunslinger and the mojo man swung atop Brimstone and Balaam and headed west. The storm had passed and the sky was open and clear. A new moon cast a pale glow upon the trail, lighting their way, despite the fact that it was nearly three o'clock in the morning.

Job looked over at his companion and shook his head at the damage the Dragoon had rendered. "I declare! It's gonna take some doing to make you look presentable again. I wouldn't expect a miracle, if'n I were you. I ain't no frigging Michelangelo, you know."

Dead-Eye nodded and allowed Brimstone to take the lead. "I'm sure Ol' Sawbones Frankenstein has some putty and paste in his mojo bag that'll fix me up good as new."

"Fixing you will be a chore, but one that I'm up to the challenge for," Job told him. "Good as new is a matter of debate and highly doubtful."

Dead-Eye sneezed, sending a splatter of black, bullet-chewed brains onto the horn of his saddle. He absently wiped it away with the sleeve of his coat. "Just plug me up and set me loose, and we'll be fine and dandy."

Chapter Fifteen

A Place With No Name
Central Texas
September 1867

Two weeks had passed since the ghostly incident at Round Rock.
    A dry wind blew across the Texas flatland, kicking up dust, peppering their faces and hands with grit. The earth of the ground was just as dry, cracked and fissured from lack of rain. The sun was scorching hot overhead. Its heat bore down heavily upon the crowns of their hats and their clothed shoulders. If there had been no garments to protect them, they would have soon been blistered and half-cooked.
    They navigated their mounts across a shallow drywash, then up a steep grade to the level earth once again. A tumbleweed crossed their path, aimlessly, led by currents of air, stopping only when a stone or sprig of vegetation obstructed its progress. Then the wind would grow more insistent and the ball of vine and bramble would continue onward.
    Up ahead, Dead-Eye and Job saw a single building with a couple of small sheds to the back of it. The structure was gray and weathered, and if there had been a coat of paint upon its boards at one time, it had long been scrubbed away by sun, wind, and harsh weather. As they drew nearer, a single sign stood at the roadside, its post choked with dry weeds and pink-headed thistle. There were no words on the face of its boards, just a single symbol. "?"
    The two riders stopped and regarded the question mark that was scrawled there.

"Now, what do you reckon that means?" asked the gunfighter.

"I have no idea," said Job. "But if that building yonder holds strong drink, I aim to partake of it. I'm almighty parched and in need of libation."

The dead man in the dusty black frock coat and hat nodded solemnly. He was once a drinking man, but his present condition—or lack of one—made that pleasure a pointless one. However, he did find solace in the cool quiet of a drinking establishment in mid-day. It comforted him to simply sit and reflect on where he had been and what lay ahead.

When they reached the building, they studied it with further scrutiny. It was two floors in height. The top flight sported four windows. Their panes were obscured with layers of dirt and grime. The bottom one held a single door and two larger windows that were equally filthy. A long porch ran its length, but there was no awning to provide shade. Five horses of good breeding and equipped for hard riding were tied to a long hitching rail. A crude sign was tacked above the door of the building. STORE & SALOON was all it said. No fancy name… just telling what was inside.

As they swung down from their saddles and tied the Morgan and mule to separate hitching posts, they noticed that eight black buzzards were perched on the ridge beam of the building's pitched roof. The dark birds stared at them balefully, perched there, waiting patiently.

"Hungry looking bastards, ain't they?" observed Dead-Eye.

The little black man nodded. "They'll not be getting a bite of me, though. I aim to have my drink and be on my way."

They stepped inside. The interior of the building was shadowy and much more tolerable than the sweltering day outside. The front part of the lower floor was the mercantile. The items on the shelves and counters were scarce, and most looked to have sat, untouched, for months… maybe years. A heavy layer of dust coated most of the product and whatever food was for sale looked unfit for human consumption.

Having no need for supplies, the two moved on to the back of the building. There, a small saloon was set up with a long drinking bar constructed of rough lumber and several tables and chairs. They regarded the occupants and found them to be few. Behind the counter stood a burly Mexican with a bushy mustache and graying hair. In a back corner, congregating around a table were five men. They were a loud bunch, cussing and drinking and carrying on. Cards lay scattered across the tabletop, but the game had been abandoned in favor of big talk.

The only other living things in the saloon were three cats huddled beneath a second table—a yellow tabby, a calico, and one that was coal black in color. They looked thin and malnourished, like they hadn't been fed in a day or two.

Dead-Eye and Job walked up to the bar. As the mojo man laid his derby hat on the countertop and mopped at his bald head with a bandana, the bartender slowly walked to where they stood.

"Mi buen amigo!" called Job with a precious metal grin. "Any objections to serving a gentleman of my color?"

The Mexican smiled and laughed. "Not unless you object to a man of my color serving you, hermano."

"Then, I shall imbibe of your finest intoxicant! Whiskey, if you have it. The name is Job, like that greatly put-upon feller in the Bible."

"I am Arturo Vega. Also greatly inflicted with sorrows and forsaken by God." As the man reached beneath the counter and brought out half a bottle of amber liquor, the table of five launched into a fit of drunken mirth. The barkeep shook his head in disgust as he set a shot glass before the negro and began to pour.

"Nasty gringos," he said softly, so that they would not hear. "Comancheros... outlaws. They say they rode for the blue coats. Bastardos malvados!" The man looked over at the tall Southerner in the black suit. "And you, Señor? What is your pleasure?"

"Haven't had a swallow of liquor since before my demise," he told him. "Reckon I'll just stand and wait for my traveling partner to finish his." He then lowered his gaze to the top of the bar and stood there morosely, his thoughts turning to other things.

The Mexican stared at him strangely, then shrugged his broad shoulders.

"You're a far ways from home, aren't you, my friend?" Job asked him.

"Sí," agreed the barkeep. "I came here to work, fell on hard times, and have no way back to Coahuila. No horse or money to speak of. I miss my *familia*...my wife and niños."

Job downed his shot. "Lonesomeness can sap a man of his zest for living, that's for certain." He nodded toward the glass and was promptly poured another. "What's with that dadblamed sign out yonder? The question mark."

"It is the name of this town," Arturo told him, "for no one ever bothered to give it a proper one."

"Not much of a town," Job told him.

"A station for the weekly stage and the only place for liquor within fifty miles. I don't own this place. The one who does, a rich gringo, he comes here every month or so, to take most of my earnings and leave me with only a pittance to get by on."

Job sipped his second drink slowly. "I know the kind you speak of."

One of the men at the corner table—a burly man with muttonchop whiskers the hue of rusted steel—let out a peal of laughter that rattled every beer mug and shot glass behind the bar. "I do tell you! I still can't get that lawman's face out of my mind! The way he looked at you when you ran him through with that big Bowie of yours!"

A tall, dark-haired man, that held the air of a commander, nodded and smiled cruelly. Compared to those around him, he was handsome, and it was apparent that he considered him so as well. He patted the staghorn haft of a large knife that was sheathed at his belt. "Cut him deep, didn't I? Opened him, navel to backbone." He grabbed the handle of a mug and downed a swallow of flat beer the color of donkey piss. "I reckon that'll teach the sumbitch to refrain from mouthing off to the likes of Garland Hughes!"

Job's hand was raising the glass to his lips for another sip, but stopped before it got there. The black man looked over at Dead-Eye to see if he'd heard.

He had.

Slowly, the gunfighter lifted his head, staring past Job and Arturo, focusing on the table of boisterous men. The black man watched as a spark ignited in the zombie's right eye and the dead flesh of his face began to stretch and creak like old leather. A great grin, toothy and damn near predatory in nature, slowly emerged, framed by blue and bloodless lips. It stretched and widened to the point that Job was certain that the flesh of the man's face would split wide open and the raw skull would be revealed underneath.

It was truly a hideous thing to behold.

Dead-Eye pushed away from the bar and stood, tall and imposing. "Job?"

The mojo man downed his swallow of liquor. "Yessir?"

"Let me borrow that pig-sticker of yours."

Job slipped his fingers between shirt cuff and wrist, and withdrew the silver knife from its hidden sheath. He slid it down the counter to where Dead-Eye stood. "Have at it."

The tall man picked up the dagger and held it in his left hand. Then he leisurely started toward the table in the corner. All the while, the ghastly grin stayed in place, unfaltering.

All eyes in the place were on him… including the cats beneath the table.

When he was eight feet from the corner table, Muttonchops stood up, shoulders squared, chest puffed out like a bullfrog. "What the hell do you want, you bony-assed bastard?"

The grin was transfixed, unnerving. "I want *him*," he said, nodding toward their leader.

"Well, that ain't gonna happen," the big man declared. He shucked a Colt Army revolver from a side holster. At the same instant, the other three stood, guns drawn. The only one who remained seated was the handsome fellow with the thick shock of black hair.

"So, you're gonna defend this piece of shit to the death, are you?"

The stern expressions on their faces answered his question. They weren't going to budge an inch.

Dead-Eye nodded slowly. "So be it."

Before the men could thumb back the hammers of their guns, the Dragoon was in the lanky Southerner's pale hand, as though it had taken on life and leapt from the holster into his grasp. Smoke and thunder filled the barroom, deafening Arturo and Job at the bar. Before the four outlaws could react, they sprouted holes in the center of their foreheads and their brains exploded from the rear of their skulls, splattering the walls with blood and clods of gray matter.

The man who sat at the table grew as pale as a bedsheet as his confederates fell backward and landed on the boards of the saloon floor with a resounding crash that sounded as one. He still held the beer mug in his right hand. His knuckles were so pale with strain that it appeared the bone might burst through the skin at any moment.

Dead-Eye's grin broadened. "Garland Hughes." He slid the .44 revolver back into its holster and shifted the silver-bladed knife into his right hand.

The man stood abruptly, knocking his chair over with a clatter. "You… you know my name?"

"Yes, sir. It's been on my mind a good, long while, in fact."

Garland Hughes reached to his hip and withdrew the big bone-handled knife.

The blade was a dozen inches in length and honed sharp enough to split a whisker hair with a single swipe. "Well, I sure as shit don't know who you are!'

Dead-Eye stepped forward, slow and easy, taking his good time. "Let's just say I'm an avenging angel," he said. "For a little boy back in Tennessee."

When the gunfighter got within reach, Hughes made his move. He drove the blade of his Bowie knife through the man's torso, just below the breastbone. He put all his strength and speed into the thrust, until it traveled through the gunfighter's abdominal wall and the liver just beyond. Steel clashed with bone as the blade scraped the side of the man's spine and the point emerged wickedly from the muscles of his back.

He expected Dead-Eye to moan or scream, or at least drop to the floor and writhe in agony. The man did none of those things. He only grinned and grabbed hold of the former Unionman's shirtfront. With a yank, Garland Hughes was being dragged across the blood-splattered boards of the floor toward a cracked mirror hanging on the wall next to the bar.

"You're mighty fond of that pretty face of yours, ain't you?" rasped Dead-Eye. He released the man's collar and, grabbing him by the hair of the head, turned him toward the looking glass. "Best take a good long gander, 'cause it's gonna be your last."

As Garland Hughes stared at his reflection, the tall man with the blind eye and a countenance like Death went to work. First he cut off the outlaw's right ear and then the left. Then he brought the edge of the silver blade up beneath his nose and sliced it away. The man shrieked and struggled, sputtering and choking on his own blood.

As pieces of Hughes fell to the floor, the three cats were out of their hiding place in a flash. They batted the slivers of meat playfully with their claws and chewed savagely with feline teeth.

"Now, let's finish this up," said Dead-Eye. "Outside."

It wasn't long before they were through the front door and on the building's long porch. Forcefully, Dead-Eye flung the man to the earth. The disfigured fellow attempted to get up, but the gunfighter wasn't about to allow it. He held the sole of his boot firmly across Garland Hughes' throat, then yanked the big Bowie from his abdomen and drove it through the man's left shoulder, anchoring him firmly to the ground.

Lying there, his nasal passages and throat flooding with blood, Hughes looked up toward the sky… and saw the buzzards staring down at him.

Dead-Eye took the silver dagger and split the man's belly from navel to nuts. He reached inside the wound, grabbed a length of bloody, gray gut, and yanked it out. Then he looped it tightly around the timber of a hitching post.

"Suppertime!" the zombie called to the eight on the ridgepole. He turned and was scarcely ten feet away when they descended, one by one, and began to feed.

As Garland Hughes screamed at the top of his lungs, Dead-Eye saw Arturo Vega and Job standing on the porch, staring at him with horror.

"Take your pick of these horses and whatever money is in their saddlebags," he told Arturo. "Then head home to your kin."

The sickened expression on the Mexican's dark face split into a broad smile. "Muchas gracias, Señor!" Then he hurried inside to gather his possessions.

"You done had all the liquor you came for?" Dead-Eye asked.

Job nodded. "I don't think I could stomach another drop. Or anything else for that matter." He scowled as he looked over at Garland Hughes. The buzzards picked, pulled, and peeled away, while the man bucked and squirmed and wailed in terror and agony.

Soon, they were in their saddles and heading westward again. The white mule quickened his pace, as though anxious to be away from the town with no name. Brimstone turned his head, regarded the bloodshed and ferocity of carrion hunger, and snorted through his nose in frustration, as though he'd been cheated of an easy meal.

They could still hear Hughes' screams a half mile away, when Job turned and eyed his traveling partner. "Do me a favor?"

Dead-Eye rode high in the saddle, staring straight ahead. "And what would that be?"

"Remind me to never cross your vicious and vindictive ass. And, if I do, give me a head start for Hell. Cause if I go, I'm walking through those fiery gates in one, solid piece… not bit by bit."

Dead-Eye said nothing in reply. He continued to ride, keeping Brimstone heading westward at a steady gait. The grin on the gunfighter's cold, dead face had diminished in length and breadth, but was still there.

Lean and low, like an ivory snake just waiting to be stepped on.

TO BE CONTINUED…

About the Author

Ronald Kelly was born November 20, 1959, in Nashville, Tennessee where he was raised a Southern Baptist. He attended Pegram Elementary School and Cheatham County Central High School (both in Ashland City, Tennessee) before starting his writing career.

Ronald Kelly began his writing career in 1986 and quickly sold his first short story, "Breakfast Serial," to *Terror Time Again* magazine. His first novel, *Hindsight* was released by Zebra Books in 1990. His audiobook collection, *Dark Dixie: Tales of Southern Horror,* was on the nominating ballot of the 1992 Grammy Awards for Best Spoken Word or Non-Musical Album. Zebra published seven of Ronald Kelly's novels from 1990 to 1996. Ronald's short fiction work has been published by *Cemetery Dance, Borderlands 3, Deathrealm, Dark at Heart, Hot Blood: Seeds of Fear,* and many more. After selling hundreds of thousands of books, the bottom dropped out of the horror market in 1996. So, when Zebra dropped their horror line in October 1996, Ronald Kelly stopped writing for almost ten years and worked various jobs including welder, factory worker, production manager, drugstore manager, and custodian.

In 2006, Ronald Kelly started writing again. Since then, he has written and published several new novels (*Hell Hollow, Restless Shadows,* and *The Buzzard Zone*), numerous short story collections, and has become an elder statesman of Southern-Fried Horror in his chosen genre. In 2021, his collection of extreme horror tales, *The Essential Sick Stuff,* won the Splatterpunk Award for Best Collection. He is currently working on The Saga of Dead-Eye, a five-volume horror western series. Book One, Vampires, Zombies, & Mojo Men was recently published by Thunderstorm Books.

Ronald Kelly currently lives in a backwoods hollow in Brush Creek, Tennessee, with his wife and young'uns.

Novels

Blood Kin
Father's Little Helper (re-released as Twelve Gauge)
Fear
Hell Hollow
Hindsight
Moon of the Werewolf (re-released as Undertaker's Moon)
Pitfall
Restless Shadows
Something Out There (re-released as The Dark'Un)
The Buzzard Zone
The China Doll
The Possession (re-released as Burnt Magnolia)
The Saga of Dead-Eye, Book 1: Vampires, Zombies, & Mojo Men
Timber Gray

Novellas

Flesh Welder

Collections

After the Burn
Cumberland Furnace and Other Fear Forged Fables
Dark Dixie
Dark Dixie II
Haunt of Southern-Fried Fear
Irish Gothic: Tales of Celtic Horror
Long Chills
Midnight Tide & Other Seaside Stories
Mister Glow-Bones & Other Halloween Tales
More Sick Stuff
Season's Creepings: Tales of Holiday Horror
The Essential Sick Stuff
The Halloween Store and Other Tales of All Hallows' Eve
The Sick Stuff
The Web of La Sanguinaire and Other Arachnid Horrors
Twilight Hankerings
Unhinged

Curious about other Crossroad Press books?
Stop by our site:
https://www.crossroadpress.com
We offer quality writing
in digital, audio, and print formats.